Stepping out of her comfort zone was never apart of the plan...

PLAIN JANE

AN EROTIC TRILOGY

TAMIKA NEWHOUSE

FROM THE AUTHOR OF *THE WORDS I DIDN'T SAY*

ISBN: 978-0-996174237

Editing: Keira Northington

Layout: Write On Promotions

Cover Design: Odd Ball Designs

Printed in the United States of America

Dedicated to

Tamika Jamison the original plain Jane

Plain Jane

"Why have love and pain when you can just have great sex?"- Natalie Jane Lorin

Never beg more than once

I gripped my cell phone as if it was the lifeline to his hello. Speak to him Natalie. Just say something to change his mind. I was too prideful at this point. I had nothing more to give and I was tired of being in love alone. I dropped my head into my left hand and studied the cell phone that I clung to in my right hand.

"Do you love me?" I asked Kenneth. Isn't it funny how the one name that used to give you butterflies was now like a bucket of crabs? They just disgusted the hell out of you.

He avoided the question and continued his rant about how unhappy he was and how he was tired and needed a break. I would be lying if I said I didn't see this coming and that I halfway didn't give a fuck. But I did. He was familiar. He was security for me. He was easy. He was all that I had known.

"Natalie, listen to me. Just give me a moment to figure some things out; then maybe we can talk more." He hung up so fast that I didn't get a chance to respond.

I fell backwards onto the bed and stared at the ceiling fan. I told myself not to cry, but I could feel the warm tears fall back and land inside of my ears. I winced at the pain in my chest, from a broken heart. I turned my head to the right, looking at the TV that was on, but was on mute and stared at that. I didn't blink for minutes at a time and felt that my breath returned to my body, only to give me air to live.

Kenneth was my everything. He was my husband. He was my life. But what was I to him? I felt replaceable to him, and he was making it very clear that I was in fact, not his everything.

Walking into my bathroom, my feet touched the cold marble floor as I rose up on my tippy toes until my skin was familiar to the chill. I planted myself in front of the mirror and stared at my reflection. My eyes were swollen and dark, my lips were quivering; my eyes traveled to my dark skin, my shoulders, my full breasts, my slim waist, and I turned to the left to catch a view of my peach-shaped ass. I was fly no doubt. But something was missing. All of me didn't keep my husband here.

My eyes shot back up to my hair. I had been growing it since I was fourteen; the year that I had met Kenneth. My hair was so long now that it was hard to manage and I had always wanted to cut my brown tresses. But Kenneth loved my length. He was amazed that a black woman's hair, especially a chocolate one, could grow down her back.

I frowned at my hair and began to pull out drawer after drawer. Not finding what I was looking for, I rushed down the stairs of my house and rushed into the kitchen. Opening the knife drawer, I pulled out the sharpest knife, grabbed a handful of my hair and in one quick move, I sliced my hair off; one handful after the other. In mere seconds, I looked down, saw the floor covered in hair, and I fell down on my knees, crying.

I cried for what seemed like hours, but were only minutes. Never cry over a man, you just get under a new one. I heard Mama's voice in my head and suddenly felt like she was in the kitchen, staring at me and shaking her head. I stopped crying. I stood up slowly and took a deep breath.

I picked up the house phone and dialed Destani. "Hey girlie, what's up?"

"Can you fit me in? I need my hair done."

"Sure mama, when you wanna come?" I could hear Destani's ghetto butt popping her gum as she asked her question.

"I'm coming now. I need a whole new look. And I am going to need it by tonight."

Chapter 1

Joyclyn Jones

Her Name is Joy

"You remind me of a love that I once knew. Is it a dream or is it déjà vu. I just had to let you know so that I can sing it."-Mary J. Blige

I was staring and I didn't mean to. No, I didn't want to, but I couldn't take my eyes off her change. I had taken to this particular Starbucks for three months now, not just for the coffee, but also for her. The shy dark girl that always had her nose in her laptop. She would sip on her latte or eat a muffin for hours at a time, sometimes. I had managed to get in some small talk with her, but only a few times. I liked to think she hid behind her hair. This long, brown, beautiful bush that was naturally curly, like some afro queen '70s type trend. Her dark skin was addictive, smooth, and had a rich chocolate appeal to it. I was in awe. I was fascinated and she had no idea the thoughts that were running through my head.

I push back my chair and walk over to her. "Hey!" I didn't waste any time speaking, as I demanded her attention and took a seat at her table.

She had on these blue nerd-type frames and her hands were gripping a novel that I was sure was more than four hundred pages. "Hey, Joy right?"

She smiled at me as she called my name and my stomach fluttered. "Hey Natalie. I was just sitting over there and looked up and noticed your hair."

Natalie bashfully took her hand up and brushed the back of her head. It was cut short. Extremely short. "Oh yeah, I decided for once I wanted to see the back of my neck." She joked.

It changed her look. From beautiful to gorgeous. I was just in awe and couldn't believe that a haircut could change someone's look so much. "I needed a change." She added.

"I see and I love it girl," I said in the best home girl tone I could muster up. "It makes you look like Lupita Nyong'o."

She beamed and said, "My homegirl Destani said the same thing after she finished cutting it."

I reached to touch the back of her head. "She did a great job." I cupped her head slowly and studied her. Her breathing slowed, but deepened as she took a deep breath and began to stutter her next sentence.

"So...so...yeah...you're working on something today?"

Each time Natalie saw me in here, I had my nose buried in my laptop, but I was never looking at anything special. I was always focused in on her and I think I finally knew why.

"No I just came in for a latte, you're reading...."I lifted her book and saw the author, "Jackie Collins' novel, huh?"

"Yes ma'am. Love her."

"So where is one headed to with a new fresh look like yours?"

"Home after Starbucks closes." She then mumbled something under her breath. From my calculation, she didn't want to go there, but it seemed that was the only optional destination.

"How far do you stay from here?"

"Just about ten miles."

I rose up and clasped my hands together. "Then its settled. You will go home and change and then come out with me."

"Go out, wait?"

"Why haven't any of your friends taken you out, looking as good as you do girl? Let's go roam these Atlanta streets. I know a few things we can get into."

"I just haven't felt like doing anything really."

Something about her eyes said she was going through something. I sensed uncertainty, but at the same time, I was good at reading people and she was curious about what I had in mind.

"Look; we've sat here across from each other for months now. You know my name. I know yours. Let me show you out. I don't know too many people here and it would be cool to get out and loosen up,

4

and not be doped up on lattes all the time." I laughed.

She places her bookmark in her book and pushed back from the table. "Fine, fine; let's go."

Chapter 2

Natalie Jane

Get on your knees

"Both of us are mad for nothing. We won't let it go for nothing. I know that sometimes it's going to rain; but baby can we make up now because I can't sleep through the pain."- Ne-Yo

Unlocking the door to my home, I allow Joy to follow in behind me. I turn on the living room light and make my way into the kitchen. "Want something to drink while you wait?" I called out.

"What do you have?" Joy replied.

"Wine, some juice, grape soda, because you know every black home has to have something grape." I laughed.

Joy laughed out and said, "Shiddddd, give me the grape soda, lady." I grabbed a soda pop and tossed it to her.

"So where is this special place of yours?" I stood in the doorframe of where the living room and kitchen connected and leaned against the frame.

"Well, I am a sucker for R&B and I figured we could go to this dance type place that has like live music and they do line dancing. I figured we could dance, drink, hit on some potential cuddy buddies and call it a night."

"Cuddy buddies?"

"Yeah girl, it be a lot of cute guys there."

I looked at her curiously and quizzed her again, "I don't know if I am ready for all that."

After taking a sip of her drink, Joy asked, "I was about to ask the where is he question but you can go right into it."

"He?"

"Yeah the man in these pictures around the room. Your husband?"

My eyes traveled across the room and landed on picture after picture of Kenneth and I. "Yeah, that's him. He's ummmm. Well, I don't know where he is to be honest." I shrugged my shoulders.

"You don't know where he is?" Joy studied me.

"Joyclyn right?"

"Just Joy!"

"Follow me up; let's find me something to wear tonight." I changed the topic quickly as I waltzed upstairs with Joy close behind. She admired my home that I had built with Kenneth. We married fresh out of high school. And it only took six years for him to walk away after that. I guess for high school sweethearts, we had a good run.

I walked into my closet. "Pants, dress...?"

"Let's show some legs, you got nice long legs lady. Got any skirts?" I nodded my head yes and pointed to where my skirts hung as Joy began to go through them.

"That red one with the gold blouse up there would be cute." I pointed.

Joy grabbed them and my gold stilettos and said, "Yes, this. Freshen up, put this on." I grabbed the clothes and went into my bathroom. "I'm going to go grab my soda." Joy called out as I cracked the bathroom door closed.

It was suddenly quiet enough to think. What are you doing going out? You should be home, waiting on Kenneth to call. I stared at my new reflection, rubbing my hair as if magically my locks that I had butchered would suddenly reappear.

Staring at the mirror, I looked into my eyes and gave myself a weak smile. "You'll be okay," I told myself. My eyes popped open when suddenly, I had a déjà vu moment. It was a moment I would rather forget.

***

"Baby!" I heard Kenneth call my name, but I was already in bed and I didn't feel like getting up.

"Baby, come here for a minute," he called out again.

I rolled out of bed, dragged my feet towards the bathroom, pushed open the door and said, "What!"

Kenneth frowned and said, "The bonnet again, Natalie."

I scratched my head through the silk bonnet and slipped it off my head. "Better?" I asked, annoyed.

"Remember what we talked about, I want you to try it," Kenneth said, changing the subject.

I searched his face for clues when he winked and I rolled my eyes. "Head. You want me to suck your dick now?" I blew out hot air.

"Come on Natalie, just try it. Look, I'll even go and sit down." Kenneth walks past me butt naked. His dick was swinging back and forth, hitting his thighs. I blew out hot air in annoyance. I just didn't like to suck dick. It tasted nasty. How could women suck flesh; it was just nasty to me. But Kenneth kept asking and begging; so to say I did it, I thought, I'll at least try it.

Kenneth sat there watching me like a hawk targeting its prey and I could see his dick hardening. I wanted to roll my eyes, but I just kept my face blank. Just do it just do it.

"Bend down." Kenneth whispered even before I had a chance to.

"Look, don't rush me."

"Okay, okay baby, I'm sorry." Kenneth tried to calm me back down in hopes he didn't ruin it and I'd change my mind.

I slowly knelt in front of him. The sounds of the TV playing and Kenneth's heavy ass breathing was all that I could hear. I tried to psych myself out and pretend that the sight of his dick was exciting.

Fake it 'til you make it, Jane. I could hear my sister, Tasha's voice who had tried to give me advice on pleasing Kenneth. However, I was cool with the midnight hump in the night. Just roll me over, give me my orgasm and go to sleep. I mean, what else was there to sex but that?

I scooted closer to Kenneth and I could smell that he had just showered. Thank God, because the last time I was down there, it reeked of ass and burnt rubber. I bent down and grabbed it.

Kenneth jerked. "Jane, you have to grab him slowly. Sensually; like this." Kenneth grabbed himself and demonstrated.

11

"Okay...okay...okay, I got it." I snatched his dick back, ignoring the instructions and leaned in. I opened my mouth and closed my eyes tightly. I pointed his dick to where I was sure my mouth was and felt the first sense of his dickhead in my mouth.

"Ouch! Natalie!" Kenneth jerked backwards as I dropped his dick and threw up my hands.

"What now?" I asked, annoyed.

"Your teeth are what's up. You are going cut my shit up."

I frowned and said, "My teeth are in my mouth. You want your dick in my mouth. Hmmm yeah, so what's the issue?"

"You aren't supposed to use your teeth, Natalie, that's what." Kenneth now had an attitude and was staring down at me like he was halfway annoyed with me.

"I don't know why you're mad at me, you're the one that wants me to suck your dick and magically not use my teeth."

Kenneth frowned and shook his head. He jumped up and growled, "You don't know how to do shit!"

"I..." I opened my mouth to reply when Kenneth slammed our bedroom door and stomped to our guest bedroom. I plopped down and sat on the back of my legs, stuck in place.

The only time Kenneth and I argued was when he wanted some type of sexual favor, but most of the stuff he wanted was nasty. I didn't want to do that stuff. Besides, what was I getting out of it anyway?

I walked into the bathroom to get some mouthwash. After spitting it out, I wipe my mouth with the back of my hand and stared at the girl in the mirror. My feelings were hurt and I didn't understand why Kenneth was always so angry with me. Now these sexual favors he kept asking for, I just didn't understand. I wanted to cry. I wanted to scream out, but I didn't. I just looked in the mirror and said "You'll be okay."

***

I heard three knocks on the door. "Girl, are you ready or do I have to get another grape soda?" I heard Joy yell through the door.

I jumped out of my trance and shook that memory out of my head. "Yeah, just give me five minutes. I am so ready to get out of this house anyway," I mumbled.

Chapter 3

Joyclyn

The first step is to be comfortable with who you are

"Temperatures rising; and your body's yearnin' for me. Lay it on me, I place no one above thee, take me to your ecstasy.- Robert Kelly

We stepped into Rhapsody. It was sort of like being back home in Fort Worth where the original Rhapsody was. But when Atlanta opened theirs, I knew that was going to be my place to go. It was more than a night club, it was an experience. It was an experience of life, great music, dancing, and the best drinks.

"This place is what's up," Natalie yelled over the music as we took a seat at the bar.

"Two Cîroc and cranberry please. And give me two shots of Patrón," I called out to the bartender.

"Shots and drinks?" Natalie quizzed.

"Yep, we are about to loosen you up, baby girl." The bartender sat the shots in front of me. "Here's yours, grab a lime over there."

Natalie followed instructions like a kid given permission. She was greener then I thought as I studied her. "You ever taken a shot like this?"

"I only really drink wine, but hey; I am willing to try."

I laughed and added, "Let's go all out. Follow my lead." I grabbed the salt, licked the back of my hand and dashed some on my hand to where it stuck. I handed the salt to Natalie and she repeated what I did.

"Now what?"

"Okay, so now you lick the salt and have the shot in your hand, because you're going to down it immediately. I am going to sit your lime right here; once you drink your shot, take the lime and suck it. It's going to make taking the sting of the liquor easier."

"Sting?"

I laughed a little, "Alcohol burns a little. But nothing we can't take, right?"

Natalie shook her head up and down. "Wait, wait, wait, ladies. Wait for me." A voice from behind us called out.

I looked back and locked eyes in on Silk. I hadn't seen him in a few weeks. I knew him from when he used to date one of my friends. We still got along like brother and sister though. "Come on, Silk baby," I called out.

Silk leans in and kisses my cheek. "Joyclyn, what's up beautiful; how are you?"

"Get your shot. We are celebrating my girl here."

"Me?" Natalie eyed Silk and me.

"Yep, welcome to the world of karma, baby. And that ex of yours is going to wish he never left. One...two...three..." We all licked the back of hands, downed our shot and bit into our limes.

"Ahhhhh!" Natalie growled. "Oh my God, what is this?"

"A blast in a glass." I cackled. "Now drink up." I pushed her Cîroc and cranberry in front of her and as I turned to speak to Silk, I caught him walking over to Natalie and smirked. If Natalie gets with him, there's no turning back.

Chapter 4

Silk

The moment you know when she is yours

"*Apparently your skin has been kissed by the sun. You make me want a Hershey's kiss, your licorice. Every time I see your lips, it makes me think of honey-coated chocolate. Your kisses are worth more than gold to me*"- India Arie

I placed my hand on Natalie's back and gave her a slight pat. "Don't drink often?" I asked.

"Not at all." Natalie coughed. "But it wasn't all that bad."

I waited a couple minutes for her to catch her composure as I noticed Joyclyn get up and walk away. I laughed on the inside. Typical Joy. I watched her walk over to a table where a man sat alone. I knew what she was up to. She was a man-eater and I would never get with a woman like her. But Natalie seemed different. Just from noticing she wasn't a routine drinker, I knew then that she was more innocent than Joy. The way she couldn't handle her alcohol spoke volumes.

"Why haven't I seen you out around here before?"

"I have never heard of this place and besides, I don't get out much. I work from home."

"Oh yeah, what do you do?"

"I do accounting and book-keeping for a few businesses. Nothing that's exciting."

I laughed a little, "Yeah that doesn't sound too exciting. But sounds important."

She nodded her head. "Yeah, a little important."

We grew quiet for an awkward couple of minutes as I studied her over. She had short black hair, dark smooth skin, beautiful brown eyes, plum colored full lips, and her smile. Wow, it was just infectious.

Natalie caught me staring and said, "What?" Her question wasn't defensive or angry; it was more of insecurity. Then I frowned and began to wonder, why a woman as beautiful as she would be insecure.

"I was just admiring you. You're friends with Joy, right?"

"Admiring? And yes I am."

"Yes, you are very beautiful."

Natalie smiled and I know I shouldn't have, but I stared at her mouth. Her teeth, her lips, her smile. I was in awe.

***

"Buy me another drink?" Natalie asked.

I signaled for the bartender to bring another round of shots for her and me. I watched her perform the routine of salt and lime that Joy had just taught her.

"Bottoms up," she said, just before downing her drink; I quickly followed behind her.

"Quick learner," I said, leaning in closer to her to whisper in her ear.

She giggled a little more then what I saw her do before and I knew that she was feeling the alcohol.

"Enjoying your night?" I asked.

Natalie turned her head. Her pupils slightly dilated, her stare was devious and territorial. Her hungry stare made me hungry. "I am enjoying my night," she replied. What I was seeing didn't seem like a person who didn't get out much. She was tempting!

She plopped her left hand on top of the bar, held her head up with her right hand and leaned onto the bar top. "Silk..." She frowned. "Why is your name Silk?"

"Just a name I got off the streets. When I use to run them."

"And you don't run the streets anymore?" she slurred.

"No ma'am. Not anymore," I said, leaning forward and placing my hand on her waist to sit her up straight. "You are feeling that alcohol, huh?"

Natalie ignored my question and looked around the room as if she was just now realizing where she was. "It's a little hot."

"It's just the alcohol. Do you want some water?" I didn't wait for her to say yes as I turned to the bartender and asked for a glass of water. He handed her the glass and she took a few sips.

"I'm Natalie, by the way." She extended her hand and I took it just as she began to lose her balance. I turned to look for Joy, but she was nose deep in her conversation with some guy.

"Let's go upstairs on the balcony and get you some air. Plus it's a smaller dance floor up there. I can show you some of my moves. "

Natalie laughed, "Okay Mr. Casanova, show me the way to the floor."

I held onto her waist as we made our way up the stairs. Grateful that it was '90s R&B throwback night; I heard the sounds of Jade come on. "That's my song!" Natalie called out as she let loose of me and ran out onto the dance floor. I knew that any throwback music could get any woman to loosen up as they reminisced about the past.

I followed behind Natalie and went into my smooth, rocking side-to-side moves. She was grinding her hips, throwing her ass back, clapping her hands, and swinging her head back and forth. She was definitely feeling that alcohol.

I couldn't help but notice that the deep curve in her back led to a nice, round, more than two hands full ass. I lean into her, wrapping my arms around her waist and forcing her back into me as the DJ changed the music to BBD's classic, "When Will I See You Smile Again"?

"I love this song too," Natalie whispered, dropping her head back as it rests on my shoulder. I traced my hands over her stomach repeatedly, seemingly squeezing her lightly as I buried my nose into her hair. She smelled delicious.

"You feel so good," I whispered back.

"You..." Her voice trailed off. I knew what she wanted to say, but chose not to. Maybe she wasn't as drunk as I thought, because in that moment I felt she realized that she was in my arms. "Let's go have a seat," she murmured as she created some distance between us.

I grabbed her hand and took her to the very back, where the booths seemed to be hidden. I wanted some time alone with her and for some reason I was interested in her. I was curious about who she really was and why I was just now meeting her.

"Take a seat over here with me." I guided her into the booth and scooted next to her upon us sitting down. "You move pretty well on the dance floor," I said, clasping my hands together as I leaned forward on the table.

Natalie smiled, "I haven't gone dancing in a long time."

"Why is that?"

"I just don't go out much. That's all."

I found myself staring at her. The dark room and her dark skin blended together, and made it impossible for me not to focus in on her eyes. And then her lips.

"Silk?"

I jerked myself out of that trance and said, "Yes?"

25

"You're staring!" She didn't sound defensive or angry. It was as if she wanted me to continue to stare. Her voice was low, sweet, warming, and calm. I searched her eyes once more.

"Yes I am staring and I am trying not to stare, but it's not that easy, Natalie."

"Why?"

I didn't say anything immediately. I managed not to look at her and stare out into the dance floor, but I felt her touch my arm and ask why again. "You just seem familiar, you're beautiful too. How is it that I haven't seen you with Joy before?"

"This is my first time hanging out with Joy. We see each other often at a Starbucks near my house and she invited me out."

Silence again. I didn't want the impression of me to be tainted. I wasn't a romantic. I was a man who opted for sex rather than love. But in this moment, I wanted to give Natalie pleasure. I wanted her to feel something I couldn't at this moment. Ecstasy. And I wanted to give it to her in the worst way.

"You don't know me. You don't know anything about me. But I feel like I should show you something. No, give you something. I want you to understand what looking at you does to me."

"What do you mean?" Natalie raised her eyebrow in a curious gesture and studied my face. I wanted her to stop looking at me. Her stare cause my dick to harden. It hardened to the point where it threatened to tear through my pants. My dick had a mission. And my mind had a mission.

"Sit back. Just trust me in this moment, Natalie. Trust me not to do anything to hurt you. Sit back, close your eyes and allow your other senses to feel me."

"Close my eyes?" she asked again. I gave her a slight head nod. She leaned back as she was told, onto the cushioned seat and allowed her head to fall backwards on the wooden headboards.

I leaned into her, mere inches away from her flesh and whispered in her ear.

"Just relax. Breathe slow, steady, and focus in on my touch." I kissed her cheek as she shivered from the closeness. She nodded her head okay.

I eyed her breasts sitting high in her gold blouse, her breathing was so deep that they caved in and out in a sensual pace. I trailed my hand down her right shoulder, over her right breast, to her belly, and finding my way to placing my hand on her skirt. Taking the ends of her skirt into my hand, I move it up, trailing my fingertips over her thigh. She began to shake as I whispered, "shhhh".

I looked around the room and everyone was either engrossed in their own lustful journey or on the dance floor. I pushed the booth's table a few inches away from us and disappeared under the draping.

I could smell the sweet scent of her perfume dancing around in the scent of coconut-scented lotion. I laid my head in her lap and when I felt her bring her hands to my head, I quickly grabbed both of them and sat them back to her sides. I gave her a slight pat to reassure her again.

Letting go of her hands, I slide my hands back towards me and over her thighs.

I could feel the heat from her flesh and the heat escaping my mouth as I breathe in and out, creating a furnace. I brought my hands under her skirt and pushed upward, until I was now embracing her ass. I gave her a hard thrust towards me so that her ass was on the edge of her seat. Pushing her legs open with the width of my shoulders, I leaned forward and inhaled deeply, taking in her scent.

I moaned as I could hear small whimpers escape Natalie's mouth. "Shhhh baby. I got you."

Taking my right hand, I find the lacing of her panties and I could feel the shaking in her legs. That excited me. I thought of tasting her on my tongue. To be able to meet a part of her excited me.

Taking my index finger, I pull the lace panties away from her pussy, purposely ensuring my finger brushed against her lips. Natalie's body shivered as her pussy moved just enough for her cream to drizzle onto my finger.

Exposing her flesh, I lean in and kiss her pearl. I kiss it again. And again. I was giving her small pecks, each time drawing back her ooey, gooey nectar.

I could feel the rhythm of her body begin to match my kisses, as I opened my mouth to allow my tongue to taste her for the very first time. The sweet and sour flavor forced a moan as I greedily tasted her again. Sticking more inches of my tongue out, I licked and sucked, grabbing her inner thighs and pushing them further apart.

I hinted with my tongue for her to follow my lead as I move up and down, forcing her hips to become a slave to my mouth. Follow my lead. Do as I say. Spread them legs. Push that pussy into my mouth and do not stop until I tell you to. I was able to demand respect from her pussy without speaking it. As she fucked my mouth, I could feel the rivers of her cum making its way onto my mouth.

I growled, burying myself into her as if I was a man turning into a wolf. My hands dug into her flesh and as I felt her body shake in massive convulsions, I felt an explosion of my seeds splattering in my pants. My breathing was heavy, my head my lite , and as I held onto her legs for dear life, I moan, "Natalie, I want you."

***

"Ummm, hello?" She snapped her fingers in my face to get my attention. "Mr. Silk, are you ignoring me?"

I slightly shook my head and looked at her and then around the room. We're still at the bar? I turned around, looked over my right shoulder, and Joy frowned at me. "Boy is something in that alcohol of yours, what's up with you?"

"I...I...I just needed a moment after that shot."

"Apparently." Natalie laughed and grabbed her cranberry and Cîroc. "You are dazed, my friend. And I thought that I was the amateur here." Natalie dropped her head back and laughed.

"Silk!" Joy pushed me on my shoulder. "Boy, now you're scaring me. I've seen you take more liquor than that."

I shook my head and walked around Natalie to take a seat in the empty chair next to her while I pretended that I was okay. "I was just thinking about something. But nah, let's get another shot." I put on my playboy demeanor, added a little extra bass in my voice and ordered more shots from the bartender. I visualized all of that. Man no way! That shit felt so real.

I grabbed my shot and had small talk with Joy and Natalie, avoiding eye contact with her. I could sense that Joy noticed that I was feeling her too. She gave me that teasing look that I pretended I didn't see. I was tripping anyway. Natalie was just another woman, no different from the rest. I'll just stick to what I know, which is meaningless sex.

Chapter 5

Natalie

When all fails spend some time with your girls

"But you see and you know, but somehow you still neglect it. Before it's too late, boy I think you better correct it. Because you never know what ya got till it's gone. And you ain't never gonna stop, till you alone . You about to lose this strong woman." – Lalah Hathaway

"Wake your ass up. I have been calling this house since eight am." Either I could hear my baby sister Tuesday, or I was dreaming. "Natalie Jane Lorin, I know you hear me." Nope I wasn't dreaming. I growled, burying my face into my pillow.

"What woman?"

"Why haven't you been answering your phone? You know today is the women's social brunch at the Aloft downtown."

"Is that today?" I asked, stretching to search for the clock on my right side stand. It was ten thirty. "Oh shit, it's ten thirty." I jerked upward and sat up in the middle of my bed.

"What the hell!" I heard Tuesday yell. "You cut your hair off." She leaped in my bed and began to grab my head. I pushed her back.

"Girl, if you don't back up. Stop!" I whined.

"Wait until Mama sees this shit. I can't believe you cut your hair."

I got out of my bed. "Why; it's my hair, not y'alls. And I told y'all for years I wanted to cut that shit off." I walked into my bathroom and turned on the shower. "Pick me out something to wear," I called out.

"Big sis, what's up? I know you said you wanted to cut it off, but is it because Kenneth left?"

"Yep!" I causally replied. "If he isn't here, then there's no need to put up with all that hair. I never wanted it anyway.

Dang, can you just pick me out some clothes and stop with the one hundred questions?"

"Fine, but don't expect not to be quizzed by everybody and they Mama. You know black folks lived through you and your hair."

"Damn, do I have to walk around playing India Arie's theme song?" I started singing, "I Am Not My Hair!"

"Ha ha, smart ass. Whatever. It's cute though; I like it lady. You look so different. Like a model."

I yelled out as I stepped in the shower, "I am a model, trick!" We laughed. I placed on my shower cap and allowed my face to be buried under the water. I opened my mouth to allow the water to dance on my tongue to fight the funk within. As I showered, I mentally prepared for this brunch I was sure I needed, since it dealt with empowerment.

***

Spring was my second favorite season. Fall being the first. I was pleased that this April Saturday was going to ease the hangover I had from last night. I couldn't lie to myself; I was glad that I had gone out with Joyclyn.

Today's brunch was all about women empowerment. My baby sis and I were members of a women's social group that met up every season to throw a big social networking event. I merely came, not only just to have something to do, but to get clients for my accounting company. I marched over to the table where the food was at when I heard, "Hey girl!" in the most ghetto tone on the planet.

"Hey Destani." I laughed, turning around to hug my friend.

"Ooo girl, they got those wings this time. Let me go grab a few!" she said, halfway hugging me as she eyed the food.

"A few?" I challenged her, but she ignored me. The announcer called everyone onto the showroom. I followed in behind Tuesday and Destani, taking small bites of the sandwiches I had chosen.

"'Ladies, be sure to walk around the foyer to see the paintings featured by one of Atlanta's best painters. He's also walking around and can answer any questions." She pointed to the back of the room and everyone turned to see, when I recognized whom Mr. Picasso was.

He waved back and as he eyed the crowd, it was as if he had heard me call his name because he looked directly at me and smiled. I smiled. I wouldn't have ever guessed in a million years that he would be here.

"I'll be back ladies," I told Tuesday and Destani and made my way to the back of the room. I couldn't stop smiling and laughing and the funny thing was, I didn't know why.

"You got a hangover Ms. Natalie?" Silk asked.

"Just a little. I was done after that fourth shot you made us take." There was an awkward silence when we both turned back to each other and attempted to speak at the same time. "You paint?" That was the obvious conversation starter.

"William David." He extended his hand. "My artist name or I guess you can say the one my mama gave me."

"Natalie Jane Lorin." I shook his hand back.

"You have an artistic name too. I love that."

I laughed, "I've heard that a time or two."

There was that awkward silence again. "Look, I know you don't know me and although I wanted your number last night, I didn't ask. But I'm not going to let another opportunity pass me by twice."

"So you want my number?" I shyly looked away. What would giving him my number mean? I had only taken my ring off a little over a week ago. And although I hadn't had sex with or shared a bed with Kenneth in months, I was still unsure.

"Yes. I would love the opportunity to take you out."

"Like on a date?"

He laughed, "Yes Natalie, I want to take you out on a date. There's this place about thirty minutes out of the city near Lake Lanier I have been trying to get to, but I had no one to take. That was until now...if you say yes, I mean."

I stared at this sexy ass man named Silk and began to wonder about him a little more. I mean, I know we had drinks and I sense he flirted, but damn; did I flirt back? Did I give him the hint that I was loose and would be willing to have sex with him, without even knowing him?

"What is a date pertaining to?" I knew I sounded a little offensive, because he switched his body away from me and created some space.

Throwing up his hands in defense, he said, "Just dinner Natalie. I promise you nothing more."

"Ooo girl, if you don't say yes to this fine ass brother, I will." I heard Destani's voice before I even saw her. Silk laughed.

"Hello little lady. Yes, can you please tell Natalie that I just want to show her out?" I looked from him to her, shook my head and laughed.

"Why do I feel ambushed?"

"Because you are. She says yes. Her number is 404-555-2566. Call her tonight." Destani walked away before I could shut her up.

"Great, tonight it is," Silk added.

"Okay, fine. See you tonight," I said, feeling defeated. (Silk got the number but he's seeing her tonight, not calling tonight?)

Chapter 6
Silk
I never knew I needed you until I met you

"I've really been going through beat downs caught in a rut. At one point things got so bad I thought about giving up. I need you now, more than I needed you then, it's been awhile but I still need my friend." - Avery Sunshine

I sat next to Natalie, who was dressed in casual jeans and a blouse. I had told her to dress comfortably, because I wanted to take her somewhere. "You look beautiful tonight."

"Thank you. You look handsome yourself." We sat in the back of a carriage that was taking us through the hills of Lake Lanier. Natalie looked around, admiring the greenery and the moonlight that beamed directly in the middle of the lake. "It's beautiful out here."

"Yeah; I haven't been out here in months, well maybe because it was cold. But they just opened this new restaurant on top of the hill that I have wanted to go to. But before we eat, I wanted to take you somewhere."

She turned to me, her eyes sparkled and her smile was spread wide. She was beautiful, so much so, that it was hard for me not to stare.

"Are you afraid of heights?"

"Umm...no," she replied, unsure.

"I want you to join me in the air tonight. Full swing. No holds barred."

"Negro what?" she said, laughing.

I laughed out at her change in attitude. "Zip lining, Natalie. Would you go with me? Zip lining that is?"

"Oh!" she laughed. "I thought you meant sky diving or something. I've never zip lined before. Sure, I'll do it."

I grabbed her hand that rested on her thigh and squeezed it. "Alright driver, we're all set." He made a quick left turn and we pulled in front of a cabin.

Natalie looked down at my hand on hers and cleared her throat. I pulled it back and gave her a light smile, "Natural reaction."

She smiled, "It's cool."

We hopped out of the carriage and walked into the cabin. After given the instructions and gear, we set out into the woods with our two guiders. "You ready?" Natalie asked, pumped.

I laughed, "Umm yeah. I mean, I have never done this before."

"You haven't, then why ask me if you haven't? How are two newbies going to take this leap together?" she laughed.

"Because I trust that I will want to remember doing something like this with someone like you," I shot back.

She paused, tilted her head and studied me. "Either you have some great game or you got some great game. Nice line by the way." She laughed and turned on her heels, following the instructor up the tower to the zip line. I didn't respond to her allegation, because truth be told, I hadn't done anything but play the field for years. However, I was tapping on thirty-two now, and it wasn't until meeting her that I considered something more. In one day; it was crazy, but there's something about her I wanted to know. And I knew that the moment I laid eyes on her.

I followed behind her and once we made it to the very top, the instructor gave us instructions and then asked, "So which one of you would like to go first?"

I looked down and saw how high up we were. It was as if we were about to bungee jump off a bridge. "It's high as fuck!" I called out, letting it slip that I was a tad bit scared.

Natalie looked down too and placed her hand on my shoulder. "Just don't look down."

I turned to her and leaned in, kissing her. I pulled back as quickly as I had leaned in. "I didn't..." Natalie threw up her hand and shushed me. I just stood there and waited for her to say something.

She takes a couple steps near me, eliminating any space that was ever there; her eyes jump back and forth between my eyes and my lips. My breathing was so heavy that I felt as if someone was pressing down on my back. My mouth was slightly parted as if I was prepping to speak, but suddenly changed my mind. She leans in slow and places her full lips on mine.

As her lips connected to mine, I let out the longest breath ever. I was relieved as if her kiss was the air my lungs needed to help me breathe. I kissed her back, taking my hands and pushing her belly up against my belly.

Natalie pulls back and smiles, "I'll go first." She pushed back and leaps off the platform so fast; I didn't have time to reply or even time to react. She kissed me in a way I had never felt before and as I watched her fly through the air down the zip line and disappear out of sight, I knew then that I never wanted her to leave my sight. Never.

Chapter 7
Natalie
Let's play follow the leader

I was trailing behind Joyclyn like a puppy. Shoot, I was a puppy. I wasn't sure about my decision to follow her here. After my date with Silk, we've talked on the phone every day since then. Not just every day, but all day long. And when I realized what I was doing, that I was getting to know someone new, I grew frightful. I didn't admit to anyone aloud, but I knew why Kenneth left. I couldn't please him.

"You ready, girl?" Joyclyn was dressed in a long red coat. I was in a black one a little similar. It was only yesterday we were having a conversation about my moving on from Kenneth. She expressed this club she was a part of.

"Ready as I'll ever be."

"Remember, it's your first time. All you have to do is watch." I nodded my head okay and followed in behind her.

The bouncer greeted us and said, "ID's ladies." I showed him mine. We walked into a slightly lit room and I followed behind Joyclyn.

"We can check our coats in over here," she ordered.

"I have to take my coat off here?" I asked, unsure.

"Yes, are you okay? Trust me baby girl, it's not scary at all. You're with me anyway. We'll stay together." I nodded my head and followed in behind her.

I watched her take off her coat and I followed suit. She gave me a head to toe. "Finally, I see what's up under there. Sexy lady. I love it." I looked at the nearly see-through negligee I had on and smiled bashfully. "Here, take one of these masquerade masks and place it over your eyes and nose."

I did as I was told. Joyclyn grabbed my hand and pushed open the door that I was certain led to the main room, where I would see only God knew what. I squeezed her hand tighter and followed in behind her. Making a quick right, walking down a long hallway and then another right, revealed what I had only envisioned. I was about to witness people have sex for the very first time.

Chapter 8
Joyclyn
Ask and it shall be shown to you

I was like a madam showing her new baby the ropes. Don't get me wrong; I wasn't about to pimp Natalie. I was just going to show her my world. The fact that her husband had just left her, made her easy and curious about my world. She wanted a distraction from her heartbreak and I appointed myself to be that very thing she needed. She needed a new life.

I gave Natalie a gentle tug on her hand to get her attention. I mean; with all the naked ass everywhere, I was sure she struggled with not staring at all. "You good?" Natalie nodded her head, but her face said otherwise.

I led her to a back room called, "Cierra". It was the room that many people could watch or participate. I knew that I couldn't get Natalie to participate on this go-round, but I definitely was going to give her something to watch.

"Take a seat right here. Don't move."

"Okay, but where are you going?" Natalie grabbed my hand.

I pointed across the room. "You see that guy over there?" She nodded yes. "I'm bringing him back over here. Hold tight." I scurried off before Natalie could ask any more questions as I made my way over to Lyndon. He and I had never been more than fuck buddies and have had quite the sexual appetite together. When I called him to say I had fresh fish to break in, he was down for it. Tonight, Natalie was going to get a show she would never forget.

***

I slowly and seductively dance in front of Lyndon. His six foot three frame towered over my five foot six body and playfully slapped my ass. "Bring your sexy ass here," he demanded. I laughed, allowing my body to be thrown into his.

"Hey Daddy!" I purred.

Bending down, Lyndon sloppily kisses my lips, pushing me backwards onto the chair that sat mere inches away from Natalie. "Hmmm," I moaned as my ass connected to the seat. My lace see-through negligee wasn't any shield for my hardened nipples that were now pushing through the fabric. Lyndon notices them too, takes his teeth and bites the left one.

"Ouch!" I playfully screamed, pushing his head into my breast. I shake them back and forth, as he pulls the lace top from my torso, revealing my naked and erect nipples. "Hmmm, Daddy."

I could see Natalie watching. She hadn't turned away and that meant one thing. She was interested in what she was seeing. I grab my legs, throwing the mound of my pussy into the air for Lyndon to get a good view. My pearl was swollen and pushing its way between my lips, calling out, "Taste me Daddy; I want you to taste this pussy."

Lyndon took to his knees and as if he were in a position to say a prayer, he opens his mouth, sticks his tongue out, and dips it inside of me. His tongue was in the form of an L as he draws back my pussy's nectar, creating a natural lip balm for his lips. I looked down to watch the show as he dipped in and out of my pussy while my ooey, gooey, cream oozed. I could see the evidence of my cum drizzle down his tongue like cinnamon frosting.

I jerk my head back as I pulled my legs back further to my belly, thrusting my hips into Lyndon's mouth. When I felt myself coming, I called out, "I'm about to cum." I eyed Natalie to see if she was indeed watching and she was. I squeezed my eyes really tight and allowed my head to fall back once more when I felt my pussy squirt out juices. "Ahhh!" I screamed.

Lyndon greedily buried his face in my juices as we both breathed in and out deeply. "Let me taste you, Daddy."

Dropping my legs, I stood up; my knees wobbling from my orgasm as Lyndon wiped his face with the back of his hand. He planted himself in the spot I was just seated in as I looked over to Natalie. "Come here, baby girl. I want to show you something."

Natalie's eyes were big as if she were in shock. I wanted to laugh, but I held my composure. I was certain that Natalie had never squirted before as I did and wondered how the hell that could come out of me. I would explain later, I thought. "Get on your knees," I order her.

"On my knees?"

I nodded my head slowly. "You're not going to touch or do anything. I just want you to be able to see well. I want you to get a good view of what I am about to show you. Pleasing your partner is very important, baby girl. You should know that sex isn't about yourself, it is an experience between two beings whose main goal is to please each other." She nodded her head slowly.

I pointed to a spot on the floor. "Kneel here. I am going to kneel next to you." I took a spot on the floor and waited for Natalie to follow me. Natalie took to her knees and kept looking back from me to Lyndon, who lay back on the chair.

"Never mind who he is. He is a willing partner that's going to help you see."

"Help me see what?"

"How to please a man with your mouth!"

"You are going to suck his dick, right here?" I wanted to say, didn't you just see this nigga eat my pussy and I nut all over his face? Of course, I am going to suck his dick. I want to show him appreciation for my nut, dammit. But I didn't. I just nodded my head yes and placed my index finger to her lips to quiet her.

I glanced at Lyndon and then eyed his dick. His dick was beautiful, nine glorious inches. He had a long, black and purple dick too, with the cutest pink head. My mouth began to salivate with the thought of tasting him and pleasing him. I took my right hand and began to stroke him.

"Touch him first and stroke him gently. Let him know that you are preparing for him, but you want him at full salute." Natalie began to reach in as if I were telling her to stroke him. I shook my head. "Baby girl, watch me."

She pulled her hand back and shook her head okay. "You want him to block everything out. You want him to only think about you, your hands, your mouth, your body. If his mind wanders, you don't have him."

"Sometimes you can open your mouth as wide as you can and go right into sucking. But tonight, I want to take my time. Tonight, I want to please his body as well as his mind. Always remember, the more you do, the more you touch, the more you pay attention, the more of his mind you have. You can control every part of his body in that moment."

I leaned forward, coming face-to-face with Lyndon's dick, smile deviously, and push my lips together, blowing out gently so that my cool breath trailed across his erect flesh. I peck the tip of his head with my full lips one time, then again, and once more. With each kiss, I opened my mouth slightly, allowing the wetness of my mouth to leave traces on his head. Lyndon hardened with each kiss as he grew and extended each second in my hand. I release my grip I had on him, allowing the tips of my lips to hold his dick in place.

I extend my jaws as far as they could open and took in two inches. I breathed deep and took in another inch, another inch, and then another inch. Arching my back and angling my neck straight, I took the depths of him to the back of my throat, closed my mouth shut and moaned. The tension in Lyndon's body began to loosen as he dropped his head back. I push back, releasing a few inches out of my mouth, only to drop back down and suck him back in.

Opening and widening my mouth, I trail my tongue around his shaft and pull back as I moistened my mouth with saliva. I moaned with each suck, each lick, and with every stroke of my tongue. Popping my lips, I pull Lyndon's dick completely out of my mouth to focus in on his head. His sensitive spot. Opening the slit in his dick, I dip the tip of my tongue in and out; in the same rhythm, Lyndon dipped his tongue in and out of my pussy earlier.

I bobbed my head in a fast rhythm as Lyndon joined in on the dance. I moaned when he moaned as he grabbed the back of my head and motioned that he wanted my mouth. Opening wide, I obey his request and bury him inside of me. Lyndon growled and moaned as he jerked his body up and down.

"Ahhhh!" Lyndon's warm seeds began to escape inside of my mouth. I kept rocking. I kept moaning, making sure I sucked every drop of his seeds. "Damn baby!" Lyndon huffed and puffed as I wiped my mouth with the back of my hand.

A couple of minutes passed as Lyndon and I caught our breath, then as if we were in sync, we turned and looked at Natalie and said, "Your turn."

Chapter 9

Natalie

My very first time

Is that what coming looks like?

Kenneth never stuck his tongue inside of me like that. Damn, what this man is doing? I have never experienced... Oh my God!

Oh my goodness his dick is big.

She opened her mouth so freaking wide, okay, now I get it. That's how you don't use your teeth.

Is she sticking her tongue inside of his dick?

"Your turn." I eyed them both back and forth as my mouth hung low. I thought I was going to watch. I didn't think I was going to be doing anything. I don't know about this. I think I should get out of here.

"But you said I didn't have to do anything," I questioned Joyclyn.

"Trust me when I say I am keeping my word. We won't even touch you."

I looked at her as if I were challenging her word. I figured I was a grown-ass woman; if they tried something I didn't like, I would just get up and walk away.

I took a seat in the chair that suddenly seemed to be a historic chair. I was witnessing and seeing all sorts of stuff for the first time. What was about to happen to me? I felt like this chair was made of magic or something. I could feel myself getting excited with jitters as I tried to hold back my emotions. I didn't want to seem immature.

"Lay back, relax. Imagine I am not here," Lyndon assures me.

I shook my head nervously as Joyclyn rubbed my thigh to relax me. "Close your eyes. Listen to the sounds of passion around you." I did what I was told. "Channel your other senses, baby girl. Focus in on your sense of touch, your hearing, and what you can smell." I heard moans and screams, through the sound of the music being played. I could feel the warm stiff air and smell what I knew was the aroma from people having sex.

I close my eyes and rested my head on the back of the seat. "Take your legs in each arm, baby girl, and pull them back to your chest."

Again, I did what I was told. Keeping my eyes closed, I pulling my legs back towards my chest. Slowing my breathing, I told myself to relax. "You are beautiful," I heard her say. I could sense the heat from her body close to mine, but I couldn't see her. I couldn't touch her. I had no idea exactly where she was, or what she was looking at. Is she going to touch me? Is he going to eat me like he did Joyclyn? I had a hundred questions going at the same time as I felt someone move over to my right. With my pussy pointed straight in the air, I began to feel self-conscious.

She moaned and whispered in my ear, "The most powerful tool you possess is staring back at us right now. Beautiful, wet, and fat. Open your legs wider. Let her breathe. Let her see what's around us." It was weird, but I began to think of my pussy being a completely different person. I spread my legs further apart, pull them back closer to me and held onto my legs for dear life.

What was next; what was next?

I felt pressure down there. It felt as if someone was placing pressure on my pussy and pushing it down, but no one was touching me as far as I knew. It grew hotter and the anticipation was driving me insane. I then heard Lyndon moan, but his sound seemed further away. I could feel Joyclyn move away and suddenly I sense her down there, towering over me when she said, "Hey pretty pussy. Baby girl, she is staring right back at me."

In a split second, I felt wind blowing directly on my pussy and then hot air. Then cold air again. That's when I realized it was Joyclyn, blowing air from her mouth and I began to shake. Not a normal shake either, but I couldn't control it. It was heated, it was pressure, and I jerked and squirmed, and let out a big shout. "Oh my God, oh my God, what just happened?"

I popped my eyes open to search for Joyclyn and Lyndon, who were both standing over me with devious grins, if you ask me. "That baby girl is making the pussy come without even touching her." I dropped my mouth in shock and covered my mouth. That was an orgasm?

To feel like that without even being touched blew my mind. And I dangerously wanted more of that feeling.

Chapter 10
Natalie
A million and one questions

"Your love is like one in a million. You give me a really good feeling all day long." - Aaliyah

"I would like to think that you were happy." I turned to my big sister Tasha, who was in town from L.A. and eyed her. I wasn't prepared for her judgmental tone as she examined me from head to toe. "The cut is sharp on you though."

"You have any more questions for me, Tasha?" I was annoyed and I knew my attitude was apparent.

"Don't get an attitude with me. Now when we get to Mama's house, I am certain that is a whole other story."

I shrugged my shoulders. "I was the only sister to get married and now I see why y'all didn't."

"Don't get me wrong. I have made some mistakes in my life too, shit. But, what you and Kenneth had, we all wanted. It was sweet. It was innocent."

"It got old and should have been over a long time ago. After a while, Tasha, Kenneth and I were together because we were together. Nothing more."

"Where is he at now?"

I shrugged my shoulders again. "I haven't talked to him at all. I've spoken to his mama when she has called, but the last time we spoke now was about a month ago. I know he's with someone else. Supposed to be in Florida, I think."

"Florida?"

"Yeah!"

I watched Tasha make a right turn after exiting the highway and glance over to me. "Why are you so calm about this? Am I missing something?"

"Am I supposed to be crying and depressed? Nah, I'll leave that to you and Tuesday. I ain't getting depressed over any man. Hell, even Mama did that behind Daddy when he left. I am just glad Kenneth and I didn't have any kids together."

"Shit, I guess not, huh? You way better than me. Y'all was together for years though."

"We just lived together. The love had been gone." I shocked myself with how easy the truth slipped out of my mouth. I was finding my own way of moving on, but I just couldn't tell anyone just how that was.

In a matter of minutes, we were pulling in front of Mama's house. Along with a dozen cars outside Mama's house, I saw a couple of my uncles on the porch. I blew out hot air as I prepared myself to be asked a million and one questions about Kenneth, am I okay, my hair being gone, and whatever nonsense that was about to come my way. Then I thought, dang, I should have driven in case I wanted a quick escape.

We hopped out of the car and my uncles waved us over. "Tasha is that you and who that other woman?"

"It's me, Uncle Elroy." I called out,
"Jane."

"Natalie Jane, is that you?" My
Uncle Elroy squinted his eyes and stared
at me. "Child, where is yo hair at?"

I laughed, hugging and kissing him
and then his brother. "I cut it off, Uncle.
It's the new style."

"But you had them white people
hair. The good hair."

"I still have good hair now, just
shorter," I assure him. I patted him
quickly and dodged another question
quickly, as I rushed inside and left Tasha
to talk to them.

"Hey everybody." I had an agenda
for yelling out loudly. I wanted everyone to
see me now at once and get the questions
over with. I got more compliments then I
expected, as I hugged a few cousins and
aunties. "Where's Mama?"

"In the kitchen, child; you know
how she will cook all day long," one of
Mama's friends said.

I walked through the living room
and into the kitchen "Hey Mama." I was
mad at myself. I hadn't come over in a

couple months, because I was lost in my own world that was changing and the new life that Joyclyn was introducing me to. I hadn't come to see my mama. She turned and smiled at me, "So you out of hiding now?" She walked over and popped me on my behind.

I laughed out, "Yes ma'am." She brushed the back of my hair and mumbled something before walking away.

"Finally cut it off, huh? Good!" I stared at her curiously and was clearly lost. "Your hair, child, don't look at me like you don't know what I am talking about. You've wanted to cut that hair of yours forever now. But that husband of yours wanted you to wear it like it was some damn trophy. Oh trust me; a mother knows all. And I knew you didn't want all that hair."

I laughed slightly though as I was still calculating what my mother was telling me. "You knew I wanted to cut my hair?"

She waved her hand at me. "I know everything and I am happy to see you smiling, baby."

"Thank you, Mama." I walked back over to her and kissed her cheek.

"Where's Tasha and Tuesday? I ain't cooking all this food for my health now."

"Heyyyyyyyyy Mama!" Tasha's loud voice bounced off the kitchen walls. Mama dropped everything in her hand and nearly ran over to Tasha. This was the first time she was seeing her this year.

I sat down on the bar stool to watch the reunion, when I felt my phone buzz. "Hey!"

It's him. I smiled and began to text back. "Hey you." I hadn't managed to get a second date with Silk yet, and I was patiently waiting. "When can I see you?"

"Is tonight good? I have an art show I have been preparing for that has been keeping me busy, but the opening is tonight. I would love for you to come."

"Can I bring my sister? She likes art, and she's in town. I can't ditch her."

"Yes, bring her. Shoot, bring the whole family if you want. LOL. I need to see you."

"Okay, lol. I will see you tonight. Can't wait."

"Me either!"

***

I was dressed in a lemon-colored sundress. I grew about two inches with my wooden heel sandals that were the home to my pink-colored toes. I went to Destani for some fresh curls for my short do and was seemingly sporting a curly fro. Tasha wore a sundress as well, but hers flowed down to the floor. "This is a nice gallery," Tasha stated, taking a sip of her glass of wine. I reached for the server and grabbed myself a glass as well.

Silk's art was amazing. Some were political. Others were romantic. My favorite ones were the ones that seemed to have a hidden story. I took to those and tried to figure out what was being told. Those were the ones I felt he most connected to, the ones he took his time with because he had something deep to say. "You're staring at Mosaic."

"Mosaic?" I turned around upon recognizing Silk's voice.

"I named her that. She's my favorite."

"I can see why. It seems to be a dozen stories in this piece. One I am sure tells of a broken heart. A mother's love, and this one here I am certain, speaks to your desires. What you ultimately want...love." I stared back at him. "Am I right?"

Silk's face was blank as if he were trying to shield a reaction, but his eyes told it all. You can never lie with your eyes. "How did you see that?"

"I somehow see you," I replied. It was true. I didn't know much about Silk or William David. But I felt that I knew him in a sense that I was comfortable around him.

I turned back around to take notice of the painting as I saw Tasha walk back up beside me. "It is something powerful," she said.

"I'm William David." Silk turned to shake Tasha's hand.

She was wooed, I could tell. "The painter. I see why you paint beautifully, and you sir, are a sight for sore eyes. Yum!"

I elbowed her, "really Tasha? Can you be any bolder?"

Silk laughed and wrapped his arm around my waist. "It's okay, Natalie. You ladies enjoy the show. I have to walk around and woo some buyers. I'll be back." He kissed my check and walked away.

Tasha pushed me on my left shoulder and laughed, "Yeah bitch; you ain't mad over Kenneth, because you got this fine brother with his nose wide open for you. The way he looked at you; girl! Y'all in love or something? Who is he?"

I jerked my head back. "In love; girl please. I'm good on all that love shit. It's just something about him. Something about him that is familiar and easy. Never met anyone like him."

"Have y'all fucked yet?"

I shook my head no. "But the kiss we had was like the kiss I have waited for all my life."

"Shidddd, sounds like love is in the air to me." She laughed again. I took a huge swallow of my wine and ignored her comment. I didn't want love. I knew I wanted Silk, but not now. Now wasn't a good time. I felt that for the first time in my life, I was getting to know who I was. I was enjoying Natalie.

***

I sat down in the waiting area leading to the gallery and watched Silk say farewell to his last buyer. "Successful night?" I asked.

He took a deep breath after locking the front door and replied, "I live for this." I shook my head, letting him know that I understood what he was saying. "Great day, babe. Great day alright."

I turned around and looked down the hallway, where Mosaic was still placed on the wall. "She didn't sell?"

He shook his head no. "I couldn't let her go. Not tonight anyway. So are you ready to grab some food?"

"Sure; where to?" I said, hopping up.

"It's a Chinese restaurant in Virginia Highlands that I have been dying to try. You down?"

I laughed, "When it comes to food, I am always down."

Chapter 11
Silk

"Ginger me, with pillow talk and pretty things, ginger me, by candlelight and long walks by the lagoon. Ginger me with intellect and wine. Ginger me with kindness and cool."- Somi

She was my Mosaic. Her eyes were so innocent. Her smile was beautiful. I know people often use the word beautiful to describe someone or something, but that's just who she was to me. Just having the opportunity to sit across from her, listen to her, watch her blush and bite her bottom lip every other minute, was something special.

I, without a doubt didn't want anything from anyone, and that included Natalie. But then again it didn't. I was good on love. I was okay with sleeping alone some nights. I was okay with no one special to be there for me. I was strong on my own. Besides, love created all sorts of extra emotions that were a distraction from making money. Money never hurt anybody, well not me for sure.

"Is it good though?" I asked, laughing as I watched Natalie pack a load of noodles into her mouth.

She looked embarrassed as she covered her mouth. "Hardy, har har. Yeah; it's good, shoot," she finally responded after swallowing her food. She took to her plate to prepare another bite. "Females make me laugh sometimes. I can't sit here and eat cute when I'm hungry."

I laughed at her; she seemed real and down to Earth. "I guess you are right about that. I'm with you." I loaded up my fork with pasta as well and stuffed my mouth while humming. She laughed.

I watched her head fall back as her mouth opened in laughter. "You can eat sloppy with me any day, Silk."

"You promise?" I didn't hide the fact that I was flirting with her. I added a little more seriousness and bass to my voice as I waited for her reply. I was glad a table separated us. My dick hardened as I recalled the kiss in Lake Lanier. I sighed deeply, hoping she didn't catch that either, but I wanted another kiss. I needed another kiss. I needed to make more time to get to know her. Or should I? Knowing her meant one thing and one thing only. Feelings! I wasn't sure if I wanted to have feelings for anyone. What I was certain about was that I wanted to get to know Natalie and it seemed at any cost.

"Yep; that's so! Can you cook? I can cook a little something something. Maybe we can see who cooks best, then that can be their job." She laughed, but her laugh faded off quickly as I read her face. She knew she had made a relationship joke, because that's how I took it. The thought of a relationship was apparent on her face as well, she didn't want one either.

Then what were we doing?

"That's a bet!" I replied, so that the subject could go on smoothly.

She gave me a weak smile, but I pretended that I didn't notice it.

"Do you want to see some of the paintings I am working on now?"

"Like tonight?"

"I just looked at our plates and they're almost empty. Our bottle of wine is almost gone, and then I thought about the end. And I am not ready for tonight to end."

I heard her mumble, "Neither do I."

"Then take a ride with me."

"Leave my car here?"

"Yes, leave it here. Ride with me." I was asking, more so with my eyes this time. Reading further into her. Burning a hole through her shield, I didn't plan on anything. I didn't want anything; I just knew that tonight couldn't end.

***

I unlocked the door to my apartment, which also served as my studio, and allowed Natalie to walk in first. My puppy, Pops, came running up to the door and began to bounce on her leg.

"Aww, he's so cute."

I scooped him up, speaking to him in a calming voice, "Hey Pops, how did you get out, huh?"

"He's adorable." Natalie walked into the living space and began looking around. "You live like no one that I know. I've only seen lofts like this in the movies."

"Is that right?" She eyed the black art that covered my rose-colored walls. My home was vibrant, artistic and futuristic.

"A bike that hangs from the ceiling." She pointed to the sky.

"I'm a biker. It comes down." I took to the chains that held it up and pulled down a little to demonstrate.

She looked in awe. "Why the heck don't I live like this? I should live like this. Are these your paintings?"

I pulled the bike back up and began to walk slowly over to her, "most of them are, yes."

Her back was to me as I closed in on her. Pressing up against her ass, I wrap my arms around her waist and bury my face into her neck. "Silk!" she whispered.

I didn't respond immediately. I knew that she was probably fighting the urge to be near me. "Yes!" I whispered back.

"I don't..."

Her voice trailed off as I hugged her tighter. "You smell wonderful, babe."

She brought her hands up to mine and began to rub them. It was easy to have casual relationships that didn't mean anything. And it was easy to get caught up in my work, researching, networking, building my business, and to forget about things like this. Now that she was here, now that I had met her, I was lost on what to do next.

I kissed the back of her neck and asked, "I want to play you this song. Would you dance with me if I did?"

She nodded her head yes, avoiding speaking. I let loose of her and dimmed the lights, connecting my iPod to the speakers and selected Somi's "Ginger Me Slowly".

I playfully danced, walking back towards her as she laughed, extending her arms and welcoming me into her embrace. I wrapped my hands around her waist and held her close.

The melody was the guide that directed the motions of our bodies. I rubbed my hands over her soft, sweet-scented flesh. The heat between us was noticeably alarming as I felt preparation began to seep through our skin. I could hear her moan and hum to the music, burying her face into my chest. It was then that her five foot six frame seemed smaller, in need of nurturing, and I was open to being that comforter for her.

I took two steps forward, pretending that I was initiating dance moves as I eyed my wine-colored couch. I was touching every part of her, as we grew closer. Creating space between us, I look down, grabbing her chin and forcing her head upward to gain easy access to her lips. Our eyes speaking to one another as her mouth slightly parted. I could see the rise and fall of her chest as her breathing sped up.

I could hear her begin to speak as I greedily covered her mouth with mines. Her full lips became a slave to my quest to make them mines. I wanted to consume every inch of her mouth. Grabbing her waist, I pulled her into me as I pushed us backwards, and slowly laid her back down on the couch.

Cupping her ass, I wrapped her legs around my waist and nuzzled myself within her. Her hands grabbed the back of my head as she pushed me further into her mouth. Seconds passed and minutes became evident as we became lost in this kiss. The kiss. Better than the last time.

I pulled back from her in such a rush that our bodies jerked. Now leaning upward, we stared into each other's eyes, our breathing rapid and aggressive, our bodies still wrapped within each other. I took my right hand, brushed her cheek, allowed it to run down her neck, over her breasts, and landing at her belly button.

I whispered, "Natalie..."

Chapter 12

Natalie

Without the penetration

"Some say the X make the sex get spectacular, make me lick you from yo neck to your back, then you're shivering, tongue delivering. Chills up that spine, that ass is mine. Skip the wine and the candlelight, crystal tonight." – The Notorious B.I.G.

I felt as if this man was speaking to me without even having to say a word. What was he doing? Why was he kissing me like this? I watched him study me as if I were a mystery he needed to solve. Hell, this moment was a mystery, but what I did know was that my body was reacting to him in such a way I had never felt before.

"You are something beautiful, Natalie."

I shivered and purred at the sound of my name rolling off his tongue. I had to take my eyes off him and look down at my kitty with one eyebrow raised. The pulsation and the pressure down there was beginning to be unbearable. It was pulsating so much that I had to see if you could see it move up and down.

Silk's eyes followed mine as he scooted out of my entrapment and slid further down. The music changed to the sultry sounds of Nina Simone as my head fell back onto the cushions and my eyes rolled to the back of my head. I'm in a movie. Real talk, this isn't real; I am being punked right now.

I could feel his hands grab my thighs as he pushed them apart as if he were mad at me. He acted with so much aggression and so much force that, I jerked my head back up as the words; "Oh shit!" escaped my mouth. He took to the opening of my pants and without notice or requesting, he took it upon himself to undo them.

"I want to taste you baby. Let me taste you, Natalie."

I shivered again, but this time so hard that my back arched, pushing my belly onto his forehead. He pushed me back down on the couch and shushed me. I couldn't be quiet, I thought as I eyed him as if he should know he was making me lose control.

I raise my hips up to set free my pants, he pulls them down my legs and kneels back down over me, pushing my weakened legs apart once more. Without thought, he takes his fingers, brushes them across my pink panties and pulls them to the side. I could feel the air hit my lips as I gasped for air. I felt myself go into convulsions. As I jerked and shook, Silk bends down, capturing my clit. I scream out, grabbing his head as he catches my hand in midair and forces it down to my side.

I couldn't feel my legs as I squirmed. Silk flicked my clit with the tip of his tongue and then covered his full lips around it and sucked. He repeated flicking, licking, sucking, and slurped, consuming my juices. I felt my body losing control as I screamed out, "Oh my God, oh my God, oh my God."

I screamed out, "Silk..."

Chapter 13
Joyclyn

"They say you can't turn a bad girl good. But once a good girl's gone bad, she's gone forever...I'll mourn forever. Shit I gotta live with the fact I did you wrong forever"-Jay Z

"Take my hand and follow me." We made our way through Club Chrome and found two spots open at the bar. I asked for two shots apiece to jump-start our night. "Tonight is fire!" I attempted to scream over the music as the bartender sat the drinks in front of us.

"Yes; that it is!" Natalie grabbed the glass, omitted the salt and lime, and lifted her glass. "Bottoms up!"

I smiled brightly and clicked my glass with her, "Cheers!"

"So I hadn't seen you at the coffee house this week, everything alright?" Natalie asked over the music. I didn't want her to know that my growing son was giving me hell. He was twelve going on twenty.

"Just ran busy this week, what's going on with you?"

Natalie's eyes lit up when I asked her that as I eyed her and laughed, "Is it Silk?"

She looked at me shockingly and said, "How did you know?"

"You haven't mentioned anyone else besides him, so I sort of put two and two together."

"I like him," she bashfully replied.

I nodded my head that I knew, not caring for the situation. I didn't want Natalie to get distracted from the fun that we were having. I had only managed to get her to go back to the sex club once, since the first time with Lyndon and me. She only watched then, too. However, tonight I was determined to get her to act. Oh, she was going to act tonight; she just didn't know it yet.

"That's good that you like him. But a man like that, you should make sure you can please." I wanted to dig a little more into what little ole Silk had been doing with Natalie lately when I asked, "Did y'all fuck yet?"

She shook her head. "No, and I am shocked. We have done a lot, and I do mean a lot, but we don't go past the oral stuff you know."

"Oh, so he ate you out?"

I guess I spoke loudly, because Natalie shyly looked around and shrunk in her seat. "Something like that."

I laughed, waving her off, "Girl, you are so green. No one is listening to us. It's a club; folks is drinking and trying to find someone to fuck."

Natalie paused, sitting quiet and still for a little too long, if you ask me. "And what are we doing?"

"We as in why are we here tonight?"

"Yeah!"

"To have a great time, Ms. Plain Jane." I grabbed my second shot, took it down without warning, and called out, "Your turn!"

Natalie grabbed her shot glass, at first just playing with the brim of it as she trailed her finger across the glass. She would then pick it up and follow suit. "Dancing next?"

"Dancing next." I agreed.

We hopped off the barstools and headed for the dance floor. I grabbed Natalie by the hand as we playfully danced and rocked to the latest hit song. The night was merely the beginning to a night I was certain Natalie would always remember.

Chapter 14
Natalie

"Time to save the world. Where in the world is all the time. So many things I still don't know. So many times I've changed my mind. Guess I was born to make mistakes. But I ain't scared to take the weight. So when I stumble off the path. I know my heart will guide me back."-
Erykah Badu

I grinded and moved my hips to the beat of "Peaches and Cream" by 112, a throwback the DJ played that had me acting like it was 1999. I laughed and screamed over the music so hard that I felt my cheeks begin to hurt.

Dillan was a perfect dance partner, I thought to myself. I had known him for all of thirty minutes now, but I wasn't that green. For him to be dancing with me this long and to be buying Joyclyn and me drinks, I knew he was feeling me. I also knew that I was feeling myself too, because every subconscious thing that I could possibly think about or sweat over didn't bother me in this moment.

He closed in on me, grabbing my waist as I grinded my hips as I remembered. It wasn't often that I went out to dance, but I do remember I use to cut up on the dance floor.

"I like you!" Dillan laughed out as I broke out into The Dougie.

I laughed out, "I like you too." On the other hand, maybe I liked these Long Islands. I embraced his hug and rubbed his back as I dropped my head back and pointed my face toward the sky, and allowed the beat to take me there.

"You got me over here speechless, Jane."

I brought my head back upwards and smiled at him. The alcohol was courage enough for me to look Dillan in the face and smile. I welcomed his compliments. I welcomed his touch. "Yesssssss!" I whispered.

"Yes?" Dillan whispered back, leaning forward into me as if he didn't want anyone else to hear our conversation.

"Kiss me!" I purred back.

Kiss you?" Dillan replied.

I felt the sultry sounds of Beyonce's "Speechless" in my head and suddenly, I was in the song. My body swayed from side-to-side in slow motion as I eyed Dillan seductively. I didn't know much about him. I didn't know his last name, but I suddenly found myself wondering where had he been all this time.

I felt his touch was the key to open my naughty box. I pressed my belly into his and Dillan's eyes stared at my lips as I bit my bottom lip seductively.

"You are amazing," he replied.

His six foot four, gorgeous, dark complexioned frame towered over me as I grabbed a handful of his curly hair and pushed him down to my level.

"Kiss me!" I whispered again. I felt like living on the edge. I felt like taking all of him inside of me. I had no words for how I was feeling as I felt the pressure of my clit become engorged, pushing its way in between my pussy lips. I winced at the agony of my desire not being met as Dillan kissed me. He kissed me with so much passion and so much lust, that I secretly wanted to thank the bartender for bringing these two together with their liquid power.

"You want me?" I eyed him and waited for his response.

"Yes Natalie." Dillan didn't hesitate to reply and I didn't think that he would as I felt the hardness of his dick press up against me. From what I felt, it wasn't small either. "I have a car!" I raised an eyebrow curiously. I felt like doing something out of the ordinary. The way he had me feeling was so hot, so forbidden, and so unfamiliar that I didn't want it to stop.

"Lead the way," I whispered in his ear over the music and in a matter of seconds, he grabs my hand and leads me towards the exit. I waved at Joyclyn who blew kisses in the wind as I follow Mr. New Guy to a unknown place.

***

To be in a foreign place. To be with a foreign person. To not know what to expect. It couldn't match any amount of drink that I drunk or any drug. This high was so new, so strong, so consuming that I felt my knees shake and weaken at the thought, anticipating what was about to happen.

I was excited because I was doing something I would have never imagined. I was in a hotel room with a complete stranger. But he was fine, that counted for something right?

The fact that we could do anything and be anyone to each other in this moment was pulling at me like a drug was running through my veins.

Standing in the middle of the hotel room, he kisses me as if he's hungry and the only source of food was my mouth. I desperately grab the back of his head and hold onto him for dear life. It was as if we were fighting to win the battle of whose lips would end up on top. I sucked, licked, and bit as he pulled, licked, and squeezed.

Pushing me backwards onto the wall, his hands travel across my hips and ass, giving it a tight and discomforting squeeze. He growls in between our kisses and says, "You are so sexy!"

I've never had a man look at me with so much hunger. Well in that moment, I thought about Silk. I thought about how he looked at me as if I were rare, beautiful, and needed. Dillan looked at me with so much lust, desire, and with a big appetite; in that moment I thought, I love both of those reactions.

I love to be wanted sexually, but I loved the fact that Silk saw me. He wanted to know me. But I didn't feel weird about not wanting to know Dillan. I was more interested in wondering what it felt like to have a man inside of me that wasn't Kenneth. I was hungry. I was horny. Although Silk and I had done everything but actually have sex, I didn't want to have sex with him just yet. I enjoyed the anticipation.

With Dillan, the spreading of my legs gave away what I wanted. He picks me up in his arms and throws me on the bed. I purr and cry out, "Ouch!" I pretended that his throwing me onto the mattress hurt, but it more so shocked me.

"Open them legs, baby. Let me see that pretty pussy."

I did what I was told. I opened wide, taking two of my fingers and pulling my lace thong to the side. Dillan moaned, biting his lip and dropping to his knees. I watched him stare at me and then lick his lips. "Sexy motherfucker you." The words slipped out of his mouth so low and so quickly that I almost didn't recognize him.

I lay back, letting loose of my panties, just as Dillan's fingers took the position mine just had. I could feel the heat from his mouth breathing on my pussy as my legs dropped to the side. My mind flashed back again to Silk as I remembered the last time someone's mouth was down there. I shook my head again as it was apparent that Silk was on my mind.

"Bring your legs to your chest, baby. Hold them legs," I heard Dillan ask. Hold them?

I didn't know   exactly what he meant, so I imitated in my head what I thought he meant and grabbed the back of my thighs, just as Dillan reached for my panties at my hip bone and began to pull them down. He maneuvered around my arms, sliding my panties down my legs and in a swift move; my ass was nude from the waist down.

Dillan growled as he bent down, dipping his nose and mouth in my pussy. I shivered as I held onto my legs for leverage. He shook his head back and forth, forcing the fullness of his mouth to brush across my clit repeatedly, forcing it to jerk back and forth like a bouncing ball. My ass leaped forward as if I were attempting to ride his face.

I moaned and cried out as he sucked and licked and oh, my freaking goodness; he was eating me as if I tasted like sweet strawberries dipped in honey. He sucked and slurped as if he was consuming an actual meal.

I felt that heated rush once more. The one I couldn't control as I dug my nails into my flesh and tackled its uncontrollable wave. I felt myself holding my breath and squeezing my pelvis real tight as I screamed out hot and heavy moans.

"Did you cum, baby?" Dillan asked as I noticed that he too was out of breath. I shook my head up and down as he jumped up, releasing the belt from his pants.

I saw him reach into his pants pocket just before slipping them off, and in his hand was a golden plastic square. A condom! I hadn't seen one or used one in years, but I was happy to see he had one, because I didn't. "You ready for me?" he asked.

I rose up off the bed as slowly and seductively as I could. I envisioned that I was Pam Grier in her golden years and stood before Dillan, just as sexy as she would have, pulling my shirt over my head. I then took my bra strap and released my breast from its bondages. Dillan stared at my naked body and licked his lips. "Sexy! Mmm...mmm...mmm...mmm...mmm."

I stood there, not knowing what else to do as I watched him take off his shirt, but keep on his socks. Finally, he took hold of his boxers and began to move them around. I switched my weight to one hip when I grew annoyed at the mystery and not to mention, the juices from my pussy was now oozing down my inner thigh and it felt icky.

"Lay down baby?" Lay down? Isn't foreplay over? Don't I get to see the one-eyed snake? He really needed to come on with the come on. Why the big mystery? I was horny. I was ready to be banged out, but I put on a front and pretended that the wait wasn't annoying me.

I lie back down on the bed and scooted all the way to the top as I waited for him to join me. I pushed the covers downward and slid underneath them to take away the cool breeze that kept hitting my wet areas.

I could now hear him moving towards me as I peek over the covers to catch sight of him. "I watched you all night baby. And here you are," Dillan spoke. I smiled, biting my bottom lip as the anticipation resurfaced. He sat on the bed, turning his back to me and swiftly got under the covers. He leans in and begins to kiss me again, grabbing me and pulling me closer to him by my waist.

His kisses were so fast, rushed, and impersonal; it appeared that his goal to be sensual and impress me was replaced by his obvious anticipation to get to the main course. I took his kisses and pretended that I wasn't aware of the change, and that I was into the rough kisses and seemingly erratic rubbing of my ass and lower back.

He switched his body weight and towered over me when I realized that it was about to happen. I raised both of my hands and yelled out, "Wait!"

His hot and heavy breathing was annoying as I studied him and gave him the Negro please, look. "I didn't see you put the condom on, Dillan."

"Baby, it is on!" he assures me.

I sucked my teeth and stared at him blankly. "I need to see that it is on. Trust isn't built here yet." I wanted to say, Negro, now you know I don't know you, so why the hell do you expect me to trust your word?

I could sense hesitation in Dillan as he slightly jerked as if he was going to rise up, so that I could see he had the condom on. But then he slouched back down and said, "You don't trust me?"

"Really?" I said sarcastically. "I don't even know your last name. Come on and just show me, so we can get it on." I was growing annoyed by the second. My pussy was falling asleep and my annoyance was becoming an attitude.

"Baby...okay. See...trust me?" Dillan did a swift move, lifted up, and then just as quickly, he dropped back down. Then I was puzzled and quite confused.

"Wait!" I paused and held up one finger, because I had to calculate if I saw what I had just seen. I began to backtrack in my mind. Curly hair, cute face, nice plump lips, okay; check, check, and check on that. Adam's apple is apparent, smooth dark skin, blemish free, perfectly trimmed and fit, washboard abs, the perfect V that led to his groin, but then I paused.

"Wait!" I said again. "I didn't see it."

"What do you mean you didn't see it?" he asked defensively.

I looked at him dead in his eyes and said, "Dillan, stop playing with me. Rise up. Let me see."

Dillan, who was now sucking his teeth, pushed upward away from me and looked downward, as he was now very visible for me to see. I stared, stared again, and then frowned.

"Where is it though?" I was serious. Where the hell was his dick? I saw where the dick was supposed to be. It was replaced by what I was certain was the condom, but it was hanging and the rubber looked like an unblown balloon. It wasn't covering anything. I looked from the bubble to Dillan's face, then back to the bubble and frowned once more.

"See it is on!" he declared. On what? Is this fool looking at the same thing I'm looking at?

"So umm, I am no pro at condom placement and whatnot, but I am certain it goes around something."

Dillan jerked backwards and became offensive, nearly stuttering as each word spewed out of his mouth. "Oh, so now you're trying to be funny."

I tilted my head, stared at him and then grabbed the covers and pulled them over me. "What the hell are you talking about?" In that moment, I caught several more glimpses at Dillan's member and I noticed his balls. Oh okay, well at least he is a guy after all.

I dropped my head into my hand and asked, "Why would you have a MAGNUM condom. Even I know a MAGNUM is for large dicks."

"Bitch, what the fuck is you trying to say?" he yelled out as he grabbed his boxers.

"Bitch? You're calling me a bitch, but you over here acting like boo-boo the fool with this baby dick. I mean wow, it's really small. So small I am confused on why the hell you would even purchase a MAGNUM?" I wasn't trying to be funny, but this fool is mad at me and I couldn't get past the fact that he was guilty of impersonation.

"Man, fuck you!" he called out, trying to grab the rest of his clothes. I took the sheets and wiped in between my legs and sucked my teeth.

"No, that's what you were supposed to do." I shook my head. "No wonder you didn't want me to see you put on the condom. I mean, how it is even staying on anyway?" I shrugged my shoulders as I grabbed my bra and placed it back on. "What a waste," I mumbled.

"Bitch, fuck you!"

"Stop saying that, obviously you can't!" I shot back sarcastically. I half wanted to laugh, but I figured that it would be best for me to get out of the room first. It wasn't as if he could take my kitty cat, even if he wanted to. There was no way he could penetrate me. I mean, his dick was smaller than my pinky. I could fit that in my nose. A slight laugh left my mouth as he cursed more and grabbed his keys.

I didn't say anything to him as he walked out the door; clearly, I'd just lost my ride home. I was bummed though, because I was still horny. Then I thought, let me just text Silk and see where he is.

I pressed the menu button on my phone to light the screen when I saw the notice for a waiting message and saw his name.

Kenneth's text simply said, "Hi!" Dropping my phone in shock, I fell back on the bed and stared at it. What could he possibly want now and after all this time?

Chapter 15
Kenneth

"They say if you love something, you've got to let it go. And if it comes back, then it means so much more. But if it never does, at least you will know, that it was something you had to go through to grow."-Heather Headley

I turned down my street, well the street that I had once lived on, and it felt like a scene out of a movie I had watched long ago. It was familiar, but it was foreign all at the same time. Four months. It had been four months now since that last conversation with Jane. I knew that I couldn't hide from her forever. She was still my wife and she was still very much a part of my life, but I had needed time. I had needed time to get away and to clear my head. I was unhappy. I was incomplete and I was tired of the same ole thing in life.

However, I knew that I couldn't just ultimately walk away from Jane like that and not give her an explanation. So I had to return to speak to her. She didn't reply to my text last night and I didn't expect her to. Hell, I didn't know what else to say, but hi.

I pulled up in front of our house. It looked the same. I guess she had found someone to do the yard since I hadn't. Her car was parked in the driveway and I took a deep breath, growing nervous of what will happen once she opened the door. I expected an argument, a screaming match, and maybe a fight. I knew Jane all too well. I knew her deepest secrets and fears. We fell in love as kids. She was once my best friend. So coming back, giving her another chance, and being honest were something I felt I owed to her.

I parked, stepped out and walked up the driveway. I placed my sweaty palms into my pockets and made it to the front door. I pulled out my keys and placed the house key in the lock, only to discover the locks had been changed. So I knocked lightly.

I could hear her unlocking the door and as if time decided to slow down and play with my emotions, the door opens and I see the first glimpse of her. Jane!

"Hi."

The door was only slightly open when she replied, "A text last night and you suddenly appear on my doorstep." Her voice wasn't sarcastic or angry; it was oddly calm. As she pulled the door open even more, I realized it was her.

"Jane. Wow. Hey!" was all I could manage to say. I know four months isn't a lifetime, but I had seen her every day of my life for over a decade and now here she stood; vibrant, beautiful, solemn, and then her hair. The mere fact that it was all gone and her beauty seemed to resonate off the sun's light made her appear even more attractive.

"Hey!" she replied. She stepped back and allowed some walking space. "How were your travels?"

How were my travels? I was still shocked at the new Jane as I took my first step into the home I had shared with her, but her tone, her calmness scared me.

"It was fine," I replied. The living space was the same. The photos of her and me, and family were the same. The room looked untouched and almost abandoned. "How have you been, Jane?"

"I've been good, Kenneth. So what's up? Why the visit?" Visit? I expected something more like, When are you coming home? Where have you been? Why was she coming at me like this? Where was her anger?

"Well it's not really visiting, Jane; we needed to talk. I needed to see you."

"Oh. Well okay then." She casually took a seat on the couch and crossed one leg over the other.

I studied her and looked at her oddly. I didn't recognize this Jane. She was different. She seemed more put together; her confidence and sex appeal was so obvious to me. She had changed. How? How did this person become whom I see now, in the matter of four months? I was so attracted to her in this moment; I began to question why I had even left.

I took a seat on the same couch, but a full cushion seat separated us. It was still close enough for me to smell her; the sweet scent of coconut. The oils she applied to her skin daily; I could see that was still her routine. Her scent traveled through my sense of smell down to my dick, forcing me mentally to talk him down.

"You look beautiful," I couldn't lie. I had fought the idea of her cutting her hair off for years, and in the first moment of seeing the change; it was perfect on her. I began to wonder why I fought the idea so much in the first place. It showed so much about her character. She did a lot for me. Even when she didn't want to; she made sacrifices for me and did it anyway. She often placed her feelings second and I knew that about her. I knew that she was devoted to me and that she loved and saw only me. I was her life. In this moment realizing that, I felt like shit. I felt bad for her. I felt horrible for my disappearing act. I had left her without an explanation. I had dropped her and violated our trust in a swift move as if I had not known her since I was a teenager. I felt bad; yes, this was true, but I also felt that what was going to happen was bound to happen.

"I wasn't happy," I said aloud.

"I know that now," she replied.

"It just seemed that we were just going through the motions. There wasn't any excitement. No passion. It was so boring and so regular."

She stared at me blankly. She didn't reply, but she allowed me to go on and on about my feelings and why I did what I did. "I had to get away. I felt I was losing my mind, Jane. I needed something new."

"Something or someone?" she asked, cutting me off.

I didn't reply quickly enough as she continued to talk and added, "It's fine, Kenneth. I am not mad at you anymore. I know that I should be, but you chose to leave. You chose her and you chose not to talk to me at all about it. Never mind the fact that we never had issues on talking, but you found comfort in someone else. It doesn't need to be said. I am not blind and regardless of what you may have thought, I wasn't stupid either."

"You knew?"

She didn't answer the question as she continued to say, "After years of us being friends and married, if you couldn't talk to me and give me the respect owed to even tell me what you were deciding to do, well then leaving was the perfect decision. Because you don't deserve me."

I rose up my hand said, "Wait Jane, I am not here to fight."

"I am not fighting with you." She halfway laughed. "I told you, I am not even mad anymore. We are good."

"Why is that; what has been going on with you these past few months?" I asked her. My eyes traveled from her toes, to her legs, her thighs, and as I eyed her left hand that was planted on her leg, I noticed the bare finger. Her ring was off.

I looked down at mine and noticed my bare finger too. "We have come to this?"

Jane looked at me and frowned, "This?"

"Our fingers are bare."

She laughed a little, "Are you kidding me? Kenneth, what do you expect after this time? Hell I thought you were dead and gone for all I knew. Your mama even acted as if she didn't know where the hell you were."

"She didn't. I knew that she would tell you."

"You wanted this, remember? You wanted something else. Great! Enjoy your decision," she sarcastically replied. Now I was beginning to sense a little bit of anger, I think.

"Are you mad that I left you like I did?"

"Of course I am."

I tried my best not to show excitement on hearing that she was at least mad. I needed to see some type of emotion. I needed to know that she at least somewhat cared. How could I be gone all this time and this be her reply? How could she not be screaming, hurt, and begging for answers? She didn't even ask whom it was I had left her for.

"I'm mad at how you left, but I am not mad that you left. You did us a favor. We were sinking and I wouldn't have had the balls to leave. I took a vow. I was loyal to you. I have been since I was a kid. But yes, I agree with you. I was unhappy too."

I stared at her blankly. Now I was getting a little angry. "What do you mean, Jane? How were you unhappy? Life was easy for you."

Jane frowned at me as if something stunk and replied, "Umm no, I was living a life that was boring, unfulfilling, with a complaining husband, and the list goes on. You're right about everything. We needed this."

She stood up after glancing at the clock. "I didn't expect for you to be here today, but I will be back later on, if you want to chat some more. But I have some where to be."

"Somewhere to be?"

"Yes, I had a schedule and I don't really want to change it. I've been looking forward to today. But where are you staying? We can meet up later."

I held up my hand to signal for her to stop speaking, as I shook my head in confusion. "Why are you coming at me like this? Okay, stop the act, Jane."

"Act? Now I am confused. Is there something you want me to say? I am speaking the truth here."

"Are you?" I challenged her.

"Yes, I am; I mean is there something else that you want to say? You're coming at me as if you are holding something back, but expecting me to read your mind."

"Why are you asking me where am I staying?"

"Because you don't live here, Kenneth. I'm certain you noticed the locks have been changed. My life is different. It's just not the same and why on Earth would you think that after months of being gone, I would be like, yes baby come home and come get in my bed?" She stared at me blankly as I attempted to speak, but nothing came out.

"Are you serious?" I asked.

"Very much so. So are you staying at your mom's? I know you don't want to test me and stay here. That's just not going to happen. Not only did you leave without notice, but I have been financially taking care of my own self for months now."

"And so that means I can't stay in my house?"

"Your house?

"Yes!" I replied sternly.

"So this is your house? So I guess you're going to come at me and say that now I am your wife too?" You can't have your cake and eat it too, Kenneth. That is just not going to happen with me. So now, I am going to ask you nicely to leave my house or some things will get quite ugly for you. Let's not have a fight. You don't want that."

Jane was really coming at me like a stranger. "I'm sorry for leaving, Jane."

There was silence and then she looked back over towards me, taking her focus off the clock. "Thank you for the apology. You actually could have led with that. But I still stand strong on my decision. Let's just meet up later and chat.

I'll text you." She walked over towards the door and opened it.

I didn't want to argue with her, so I stood up and walked towards the door. I badly wanted to reach up and touch her or hug her, but I didn't think that in this moment that would be a good idea. "I guess we will talk later."

She nodded her head and gave me a solemn smile. She nodded her head okay as I walked out and she closed the door behind me.

That was totally not what I thought would happen. She was different. I had to figure out a way to get to know this new Jane that was before me.

Chapter 16
Silk

"Let me take you to a place nice and quiet. There ain't no one there to interrupt ain't gotta rush. I just wanna take it nice and slow. Now baby tell me what you wanna do with me?"- Usher Raymond

I had placed a nice setting in the middle of the floor of my studio. It was more of an old small storage room that was sold to me for five hundred a couple years back. I had managed to redesign the interior and make it look almost brand-new. I custom painted the walls, one being that of a Mahalia Jackson portrait. The other wall resembled kids dancing in the street as a broken fire hydrant splashed water over them.

I had the knack for painting and depicting life that reflects my history, my face, and love. Interesting enough, love was the one thing I was not interested in. I was going to keep telling myself that even as I noticed that (noticed what?)

I heard two knocks on the door and placed the last bit of the art materials I had bought for Natalie on the floor next to the pallet.

I opened the door. "Hey beautiful." I welcomed her in and kissed her cheek. I took a deep breath as I watched her walk past me and complimented her on the sundress that she wore.

She looked around the room, admiring the walls, paintings, and bright colors. "I love this. I just love your mind, Silk."

Closing the door I walked over to her and hugged her from behind. I squeezed her real tight and imitated the sound with my mouth and replied, "I love the fact that you love my mind."

She looked down and noticed the pallet. "What is all of this?"

I took her hand and led her over. "So sometimes I do this freestyle exercise and thought I could do one with you. I get one paintbrush,   use only two colors and see what I can create, just by going with the flow of things."

"Oh yeah. Sounds like fun. Is this spot for me?" She eyed the blank canvas and brush I had laid on the floor.

"Yes madam. Cop a squat for me." I playfully slapped her ass as she took a seat on the pillow-topped pallet, took the canvas and sat it in her lap. Her smile was spread wide as her eyes followed me across the room.

"Billie Holiday is perfect for this moment."

She laughed, "I know you have some food in here too, right?"

I laughed and shook my head, "Yes baby. I got us some chicken wraps, and some sweet Merlot, so that you can paint and sip."

I grabbed the wine, two glasses and brought them over to her, and then I went off to retrieve the sandwiches. "I've never done this before," I heard her call out.

"Done what? Painted?"

She laughed and then sucked her teeth playfully, "No, this. Everything that you have set up. It's amazing and sweet and I would have never thought to do this."

"Well let me be the one to show you something new," I stated, walking back towards her and placing the food on the floor in front of us.

"I think I am going to like that." She seductively shot back.

Taking a seat next to her, I eyed the paint colors. "Which one would you prefer?"

"Hmm, how about purple and red? I like what those colors represent." I reached over and placed the colors next to her as I selected green and then yellow. She added after looking at my color choices, "They say green is a symbol of growth and harmony."

"I feel something great may be connecting and growing very soon. What do you think?"

She ran her tongue over her teeth and gave me the sexiest stare that shot a leaping force straight to my member. "I can see that," she replied. Natalie was smooth, confident, and often times I felt she knew just what to say at the right time. If I didn't know any better, I would say I was crushing extremely hard on her.

"I say whoever paints the best picture, has to do something nice for the other person."

"A challenge?'

"Yep, you down for it?"

"Ha! You can't even manage to compete with this, sir, but since you are a professional and all at this craft, I am going to try my best not to embarrass you."

I laughed and couldn't help the fact that I caught myself staring at her eyes and then her mouth. My trance was only broken when I heard, "So is it on?" she asked.

I extended my fist for her to pound it. "It's on!"

***

We lay across my floor, our canvas full of strokes and colors. Her head lay on my chest, our bellies full of wine and our chicken wraps. The music had flowed on over to Will Downing. "I think I won, because mine is cuter," Natalie debated.

I laughed, "Okay babe, you won. No worries anyway. I had something planned, just in case you cheated."

She rose up and laughed slapping my chest playfully, "Ugh, I did not cheat. I mean; my talent won. I know it sucks for you and all, but you won't win them all Mr. William David."

"Whoa, my full name; now what did I do?" I rose up, holding my arms as if I were surrendering and pretended to look innocent.

She playfully pushed my temple and said, "Nothing...yet!"

"Yet?" I curiously asked.

She lay back down, planting her head back in its position on my chest as we both stared at the ceiling. On cue, Robin Thicke's song, "I Need Love' came on. It seemed as if the laws of attraction were speaking to both of us with his lyrics;

I can do better than make love to you

Better than make you say my name
Please, please, please

123

Oh don't you make me have to beg
I need love

Silence... the quietness of the room was forcing time to slow down. I looked down and could see the rise and fall of Natalie's belly as she took in much deeper breaths. She was breathing as deeply as I was. The anxiety and anticipation of it all was wreaking havoc on me. Although I told myself that she was different and that I didn't want to rush her, I didn't want to rush sex, and that I didn't want to risk losing this feeling, I couldn't help it. I wanted to feel her.

I reached down to her and whispered her name. Grabbing her hand, I said, "Natalie?"

"Yes?" she whispered back.

I wanted to ensure she was aware that I needed her attention, so I scooted from underneath her and slowly laid her down on the pillow.

"You got me speechless, Natalie. Do you know what you do to me?" I towered over her and just stared. I had seen beauty, I had known beauty, but hers seemed to top everyone's. It was as if she possessed something that no one ever had and I couldn't figure out just why.

"No I don't," Natalie said above a whisper. Her voice was so low and weak that I had to ensure she wasn't emotional.

I grabbed her right hand and guided it over my chest to my waistline and finally connecting to my dick. I was hard; I was so engorged that I was bouncing back and forth. "You feel him?"

Her eyes traveled down and studied the area I had her hand. She opened her palm and cupped him as she slowly nodded her head up and down. I lean in and kiss her, pecking her lips.

"Why do I do this to you?" Natalie now had a good grip around me and was slowly stroking it up and down.

I starred at her as I fought to force my words out of my mouth and answered, "You...you are so fucking beautiful, Natalie," is all that I managed to say.

She leans up and kisses my lips. It was aggressive and passionate as she took her free hand and grabbed the back of my head, pushing me further into her mouth. Our tongues, dancing inside of each other's mouths, were trying to match each other's rhythm. I collapsed on top of her, burying my body in between her legs.

I pressed myself against her, gyrating my hips into her groin as my hands invaded every inch of her body. I wanted to take her body to places she had never been before and with me. I wanted to take all of her problems and place them on me. I wanted to give her all the smiles she would ever create. I wanted to do more than have sex with Natalie. I wanted her. I wanted her in the worst way.

I push her legs further apart as her dress fell backwards onto her, revealing her lace thong. Her ripe apple ass lay there squeezed between the cushions of my pillows. I went to squeeze it, taking a handful of her ass and grunted as her hands flew to the button on my pants, attempting to undo them. She wants to go all the way this time.

Our kisses deepened as the heat from my pores seeped out into the room like steam. I felt my very being was being pulled and summoned by hers. I fell into her as if I was attempting to become her and she, in turn, would become me. Her hands continued to work until my pants were finally unbuttoned and she dipped her hands inside, running her hands down as she smoothly and swiftly release my dick from it nested place.

"I...want...you..." I managed to say in between sucks, bites, and kisses.

"I want you too," Natalie cried out. Her voice had so much hunger and desire. I brought my left hand to her face and cupped it. Slowing our pace and slowing our rhythm, so that I could just look at her for a moment.

She looked up to me and smiled. I smiled back at her, closing in on her lips again; I slowly kiss her. I slowly guided her dress over her head and laid her down on her back. I rose up, slipping out of my pants and shirt. I quickly retrieved our protection, ran back over to her, and noticed she had removed her bra, but was covering herself as she lay on the pallet.

I reached back around, grabbed a blanket from the closet a few steps away and opened it up, placing it over my back as a cape. Walking over to Natalie, I tower over her, slowly kneeling down and covering us with the blanket and once more, the heat between us was unbearable.

Kissing her lips first and then her cheek, I bite her chin, kiss her neck and I bury my face there and take a deep breath. I take in her scent, leaving an imprint of my desire there on her flesh. The angelic nastiness she possessed was making me lose my cool. I was able to control my limbs and my loins, but not with Natalie.

You could hear the sounds of our kisses, the clapping of our skin connecting, the heaviness of our breathing, and the soft cries of our passion. Cupping her breast, I slid down her body, pushing her legs to the sides of my shoulders, as I became face-to-face with her pussy.

I breathed in deep, taking in her scent as if it were the first time I had met her and imagined her taste. It was déjà vu. Although I felt like this was home now, tonight I felt like she was going to provide a different meal. I felt there was a surprise in store for me as I buried my face in her panties feeling the saturation of her juices in the cotton fabric.

I growl, biting her mound as if it were an apple. She squirmed underneath me as I gripped her panties in my teeth and began to pull them downward as I slid my hands over her breasts, her erect nipples, and over her belly.

Grabbing her panties now, I aggressively pull them down, becoming annoyed at my attempt to be slow and sensual. But who was I kidding; I wanted her and I needed her now. I lean up and allow the cover to fall as I ripped open my MAGNUM wrapper and began to apply it when Natalie called out, "Wait!"

What is it? Oh man, don't tell me that she changed her mind. Natalie rose up as her naked torso sprung into the air. "Let me." She went to reach for the condom. A little anxious to see what it is she was going to do, I allowed it to slip out of my hand into hers as she grabbed my dick. I watched her reaction and from the excitement that I saw in her eyes, I knew that she was satisfied with what she saw.

I watched her apply the condom and slide it all the way down; when she was done, I leaned down, kissing her as I forced us back onto the pallet. I nuzzled myself back into her bosom. Our bellies were one, our pelvic bones were pressed against each other as one, and our breathing was deep and in sync.

I grabbed the head of my dick and pointed it to her opening, feeling her heated wetness cover me. I shivered and squirmed as inch-by-inch, I pushed myself inside of her. Her tightness covered my dick like a fitted glove, so much so that I fell on top of her, and attempted to pace my breathing and my excitement.

She wrapped her legs around my waist and held on as I pushed myself inside of Natalie. Deeper and deeper, Natalie was becoming mine.

Chapter 17
Natalie

"Bag lady you gone miss your bus. You can't hurry up because you got too much stuff. When they see you coming niggas take off running from you it's true; they do."- Erykah Badu

I walked inside Mary Mac's Tea Room waiting area and saw Tuesday and Tasha waiting on me. I hadn't gone home. I hadn't hit Kenneth back up since he popped up at the house, and I hadn't had a chance to even change clothes. I was only able to take a quick shower and put back on the same clothes with no panties on. Silk and I had been engrossed in each other all night long. We didn't even sleep. We stayed up consumed in each other, literally and figuratively.

"You ladies look good," I said with my arms spread wide, wanting to switch the vibe that I knew I was going to get from them. I was thirty minutes late and that was going to be the topic at hand.

"Whatever trick; where have you been?" Tuesday called out.

I looked around and playfully pretended as if the entire room heard her loud mouth and that I was now embarrassed. "O M G can you please be a little more civil," I replied sarcastically, leaning in and hugging them both.

"You look refreshed this morning, sis," Tasha said, standing up and walking past me to get to the host. "Our sister is here; we're ready to be seated now." She then turned to me and whispered, "You had sex."

"Ooo, is that why she walking all bowlegged and whatnot? Trick who you fucking?" Tuesday blurted.

"Shhh, oh my God, you are so loud," I replied embarrassed, as I rushed toward the host to follow her closely to our table.

I could hear them laughing and chatting behind me as we finally took a seat at a table near the back. I grabbed my menu and began to focus on that when Tasha snatched it up.

"It's that painter I saw you with before."

"When are you going back to California?" I joked. "Dang, how do you know, nosy ass."

"It's written all over your face. And in between your legs," Tuesday laughed out. I rolled my eyes at her and threw a napkin in her face.

"Shut up!"

"Oh, I am sure you would like for me to shut up. Okay, so you have to give us the scoop," Tuesday added as they both stared at me. Thank goodness the waitress came over to take our drink order.

"Okay, so answer the question," Tasha responded, once the waitress had walked away.

"His name is William David. He's an artist. Mainly a painter, but he also dabbles in architecture as well."

"Ooo, you got a Darius Lovehall and Nina Mosely situation going on," Tuesday laughed.

I stared at her blankly. "Really...you over here comparing me to Love Jones now?"

"Seems like that's what you got going on, from what you told me before," Tasha added. "You met him in a bar though, you say?"

"Yeah, through this girl I know, Joyclyn. Well, she invited me out one night for drinks and dancing. Not too long after Kenneth left, and he and I danced that night. I didn't even see him again until the brunch Tuesday and I went to."

"Oh yeah, that's right, him! That man is sexy. I wonder how many women he got?" Tuesday blurted.

"Why would you say some ignorant mess like that? This girl ain't trying to think about the others. Let her have fun. Shoot from all we know, all she has ever had is that tired ass Kenneth and you want to bring up some negative mess," Tasha said to Tuesday.

"Shoot, my bad."

I fell into my thoughts for a moment as I realized Tuesday said something I hadn't even thought about. There was a point in my life where I swore by the fact that all men didn't cheat. As I grew older and witnessed others' mistakes as well as the ones made in my marriage; I realized cheating isn't a male thing. It's a human thing. It's almost bound to happen to most of us.

I hadn't thought about Silk being with someone else. Hell, that never even crossed my mind until now and suddenly, I felt myself shrink. "Natalie Jane Lorin! I see you over there thinking. Never mind what Tuesday said." Tasha tried to assure me. "Enjoy him and have fun, that's what you should be doing anyway."

"Enjoy him?" I asked her.

"What she means is; I am sorry, sis. I have just messed with a lot of assholes and yes, most men cheat or whatever, but you are newly single. Have fun, play the game, and don't get serious. Trust me. Once the seriousness and love comes into play, the shit gets so un-fun real quick."

"Is that so?" I asked curiously. I looked to Tasha to disagree and she didn't.

"Well how do you keep a relationship fun?"

They both paused. Then Tasha opened her mouth, "He should be your best friend. Your best friend will almost always be loyal."

I nodded my head that I understood. "Kenneth was once my best friend, you know," I said above a whisper.

"Y'all were kids. A kid and a grown man are two different things, and you were friends with the young Kenneth. People change all the time you know," Tasha added.

"True," Tuesday agreed.

"So just enjoy him."

"Yeah sis. Date him. Don't ask those 'what are we doing' questions," Tasha said.

Tuesday blurted, "Oh, and whatever you do; do not sleep over. That shit stirs up feelings. And don't always be available for that nigga. Let him wait on a return call or text sometimes."

"Oh yeah, that's a good one Tuesday, because men get spoiled and expect shit from you, even if you're not their woman. There's this thing called double standards. So I say give this William David the same exact thing he's giving you. That's the same time, same conversations, same type of date, reveal yourself in the same amount that he is. Play the man's so-called game, sis," Tasha alerted me.

"This is a lot of stuff to take in. I just had one of the greatest nights of my life, and now it's all making me think of what comes with that good time, you know?"

"Oh man, baby girl, I don't want you to think about it so much. Just remember to have fun. It's okay to have feelings for someone, but don't make decisions and choices based off emotion. Let your decisions simmer in for a bit and then go from there. In any event, I got you when you need advice," Tasha assured me.

"So do you have advice about Kenneth showing up at my doorstep yesterday, before my date with William?"

"Wait, huh?" Tuesday blurted. "Kenneth is back?"

I nodded my head yes. "And something tells me he was back, hoping that I was asking him to come back home."

"You're kidding me." Tasha asked, "So what happened?"

"He knocked on the door, I let him in and he apologized, said he wasn't happy, and was back so that he and I could talk. But from the moment I told him that I was cool and that I wasn't mad, the conversation shifted. He had even expected to stay at the house."

"Wait, you did him like that?" Tuesday laughed.

Tasha cut her off and said, "So you don't want him back?"

"I haven't actually wanted him, Tasha, in a long time. It's just that he had the balls enough to walk away and I didn't. And I am grateful for that. We were just together, because that's what everyone expected after all this time. No, I didn't expect him to do me like he did and just disappear, but I don't blame him. I am glad that he had left."

"Why is it because of this William Silk guy?" Tuesday asked.

Tasha added, "Yeah; is he the reason you don't mind your husband leaving and whatnot?"

"Nope, well, he plays a part. But if Kenneth had never left, I would never have begun to learn who I am. I am enjoying getting to know who I am."

"Is that so?" Tasha smiled brightly. "That's what I wanted to hear, sis."

"So I have been going out more, I am dating which is something I have never done, and I even think I am going to start back writing my poetry again. I mean, after seeing Silk make money from his passion, the least I could do is have fun with my writing, you know."

"You are growing up, sis." Tasha patted my arm like you would do a puppy and I snatched it away from her playfully.

"Oh shut up." I grabbed my menu and began to look for what I wanted to eat.

"Let's find something to eat and get off me please."

"Fine, because you all know I would rather be talking about me anyway," Tuesday laughed out.

I felt today was going to be a great day, but that was until a familiar face walked into the room and the shock on my face, forced my sisters to look up and see who I was looking at.

"Who is that?"

I stared blankly when I answered, "Just some guy that I know."

He noticed me. I guess my eyes were burning a hole in the back of his head. He told the person he was dining with that he would be right back as he made his way over to our table. "Ladies, Natalie." He leans down and kisses my cheek.

I bashfully smile and say, "These are my sisters, Tuesday and Tasha. And Tasha and Tuesday, this is umm, a friend of mine, meet Lyndon."

Chapter 18

Lyndon

"I know you want this girl I see it in your eyes. Don't be ashamed of what you got between those thighs. You know I'm going to try not to be so excited. But I can't help it feels so good to be invited so get ready because here I go." – Marques Houston

I took a seat at the table, along with my colleague that I worked with. Seeing Natalie in the daytime was a bit of a shock and definitely more tempting than before. I have yet to touch her. It was against the rules; when Joyclyn or I brought a girl to our sexual quests together, we couldn't dabble without the other present. However, in this moment, rules were made to be broken if you asked me.

This lunch meeting was going by slowly and I often caught the glimpse of Natalie's stares as the hour passed by. Upon speaking to her and her sisters, shaking her hand hello was the only time that I had even touched her. The mere touch of her hand had me wanting to know just what the rest of her felt like.

I wish I could paint our sex in my head, but I couldn't. This woman's sex appeal was on ten and I hadn't even had her yet. I had to get her. "I think I have to cut this meeting short, Fred," I said to my business partner without even making eye contact with him.

"Are you okay?" he asked, as I signaled for the waitress to come and bring the check and a to-go box for him. I needed him gone.

"Yeah. I got the check and I will meet you back at the office," I said while eyeing Natalie, who was eyeing me right back.

She hadn't shied or looked away. Yes! She was definitely interested in breaking the rules with me. I assured my partner that everything was fine as he got up from the table and walked away. I proudly watched Natalie attempt to get rid of her sisters as well as they packed up their food.

I signaled with my head for her to walk towards the back. She slyly nodded okay.

I got up from the table after I dropped a few twenties to pay for the bill, walked towards the back of the restaurant, and noticed a back door that said storage room.

I turned the knob and noticed it was unlocked. I poked my head in and smiled. "Perfect!"

I went back to the edge of the hallway to see if Natalie was near and when I saw her walking my way, I dropped my hands to my side, as my stance resembled a baseball player, attempting to steal the home plate run.

I could hear the clicking of her feet as she grew closer, and in one swift move once she turned the corner, she was in my arms. She screamed lightly, but I covered her mouth in time, pulling her into my arms as my breathing began to deepen with lust and anticipation. Our bodies began to rock in a seductive rhythm as we stared at each other.

"Hey!" she whispered. Her lips slightly apart now, I could feel her warm breath escape her mouth and travel across my lips.

I hungrily took her mouth and my kiss became my hello. She gripped my head, allowing my kiss to deepen. My hands traveled across her body, pulling and squeezing her ass and thighs. "You want me?" I asked her.

"Yes!" she whispered.

I slid her across the wall, placing my hands on the doorknob and opened it. Our kisses were never interrupted as only the sweat and heat were between us. She rubbed my back and kissed me as I greedily pulled up her dress, discovering her panties were missing.

"Oh shit!" My dick jerked into straight forward position as I took my right hand and began to unbuckle it. I lifted her up in the air and placed her on a pack of boxes, throwing her legs over my shoulders. Taking my hands to her ass, I spread them apart, stuck my tongue out, dipped it in the crack of her ass and licked her all the way up to her clit. Then I ran my tongue back down and repeated the stroke.

I pull her ass cheeks apart, finding her hole and with the tip of my tongue, I dipped it inside her ass and sucked it. She moans and squirms as she digs her nails into my shoulders; I was certain she was bracing herself for an explosion that was well on its way.

I took my attention to her pussy hole and dipped my tongue inside of her, trailing my tongue around her walls as I scooped her juices up. I moaned and growled as I let loose of my dick from inside of my pants with my free hand and began to stroke myself.

"Lyndon, I want to feel you. Come on, baby."

Ignoring Joyclyn's voice in my head, knowing that if this encounter were publicly revealed, all hell would break loose. But I couldn't resist. I reached into my wallet, quickly grabbed our protection and applied the shield. Standing up,

Natalie lay before me, legs spread wide and her juices glowed in the dark, as I could see elements of her ooey, gooey cum.

Taking my dick into my hand, I rub its head across her lips, over her hole, and jerk her clit across my tip. I could feel her body tense up with the peak of her orgasm. Just as I knew she was about to cum, I jammed my dick inside of her with continuous bounds and strokes and I felt the rush of her nut saturate my dick like slobber.

"Ahhh. Damn baby," I said, taking my right hand to grip her breast to seal my stance. I fucked her hard then slow, dipping my dick in and out, just to tease her next nut. Her nails were digging into my waist from where she attempted to hold on.

Her moans and cries grew loud as I lay on top of her and covered her mouth with my hand. Not allowing my dick to slip out of her, I pumped in and out like a jack rabbit as I felt her about to come once more. My ability to hold out grew weak and in one hard thrust, my seeds were released as evidence that she was not going to be a one-time fuck. I needed this Natalie again.

Chapter 19
Kenneth

"Don't think twice of our love. I say these things because I love you, but it's hard to explain and I'm hoping that you're feeling the same way. You know that all of my feelings are inside and verbally I tend to forget how much I L-O-V-E U really means." – Tyrese Gibson

I walked outside and found my mother seated on the porch, with her puppy in her lap. It was slightly cooler than expected this summer morning. I had placed on some jogging pants and my wife beater in an effort to walk the neighborhood to clear my head.

"Hey Mama!"

"Morning son. I see you got some rest yesterday."

"Yeah, I'm sorry about that Ma. I was waiting on Natalie's call or text yesterday and pretty much just laid around doing nothing else."

"Oh yeah, that's right, you remembered you had a wife now." My mother didn't waste any time again. She had been short with me in everything that she said towards me, since I called her a little over a week ago. I had called her on occasion, but I honestly didn't want anyone in my family to know where I had gone.

"I am going to go back over to the house to see her again today," I said, ignoring her statement.

"I don't know if you popping up twice in a row is a good idea."

"Why is that? It's my home too."

My mother grew quiet and stared at me blankly. "One thing for sure is a woman can have a son, raise him up with all the morals and show him how to treat women. But naturally how you meatheads turn out, doesn't have anything to do with us. Once you get your first whiff of some forbidden pussy, you forget that this world is not handed to you on a silver platter and you forget your morals as a man, father, and husband. You cannot expect a woman to sit around and wait on an adulterous husband. You cannot expect a woman to love you on demand and most importantly, you cannot abandon your love and then expect to gain it back when you see fit. This isn't your world, Kenneth, and you left that girl. So look at the tables turning."

My mother pushed back into her seat, folded her arms across her chest, and laughed lightly. "Mama!" I said, trying to get her to stop speaking.

"Mama what? You want me to stop speaking the truth, son? Do you want me to be in agreement with all the wrong you've done? Hell, I've known Natalie since she was a teen and we've spoken only a handful of times since you've been gone. Because of you. So yes son, your decisions do not just affect you. Dumb ass."

"I am starting to see that, Mama. That's why I want to talk to her."

"Go see your brother or something. Give her some time. She knows you're here and she knows you're back, for the time being that is, so don't push her."

"I am back for good, Mama."

She waved me off and began to rock back and forth in her seat. "Gon' 'head and go for your run, boy. I'll call your brother and let him know you're stopping by."

***

I looked over several pictures that my brother, Channing, had placed over his house. "Your new place is cool, bro."

He walked in and handed me a cup of coffee. "Thanks bro. Good to see you back. The fellas and I have missed whopping your ass in ball at Farringdon Park. Everyone has been asking where you had gone."

I took a seat on his sofa, took a sip of coffee, and took a deep breath. "Life bro; it had me in a bind. I felt stuck. I had to leave."

Channing paused before saying, "But to do Natalie like that, bro? I mean, why didn't you at least talk to me?"

"Some things I just couldn't talk about. Still can't."

"So what now? Are you going back to work at Robertson and Bates?"

"Yeah, I had taken a leave of absence and reached back out a couple weeks ago to see about getting back to work."

"And how does Natalie feel about you coming home?"

I shook my head. "Man, that's what I can't wrap my head around. She doesn't want me to. Well, that's what I gathered. And she looked different. She had even cut her hair."

"She cut her hair, huh?" Channing laughed a little. I stared at him blankly as he continued, "You know she kept her hair for you. She always complained about it, but stuck it out for you, I guess." He shrugged his shoulders.

I grew quiet. "Yeah, I know."

"She's a good woman."

"I know this too."

"I don't know bro. She is a tough one, I mean; you know Natalie can definitely hold her ground. But if you need a place to stay, just let me know."

I nodded my head that I understood what he was saying and thanked him for the offer, as I thought about how I was going to get Natalie back to my Natalie.

Chapter 20
Joyclyn

"I'd rather be with you because I love the way you scream my name. There's no other man that gives me what I want and makes me feel this way"- Beyoncé Knowles

"You want to take a shot or two?" I asked Natalie, taking a seat next to her at the bar.

"I'll just start with one. I have had a stressful couple days. I need to start slow."

"Shidd, that's more of a reason to dive in." I instructed the bartender to pour us two shots. "So what happened today?"

"Well, within the past twenty-four hours, I have managed to come face-to-face with two men in a way that I have never expected. I actually slept with Silk. After that, the dog came knocking on my door."

I was a little bothered hearing about Silk and her smashing, but then I questioned, "Dog?"

"Kenneth!"

"Oh him. So he came back home, huh?"

"Huh my ass, he will never get me like he had me before. I am not that same person. I am not going to beg and plead any man to stay or to talk to me," she preached. I knew that she was feeling some type of way as she downed the shot without so much as a toast or a warning.

"So Silk, huh?" I changed the subject.

The mention of his name caused this glow in her eyes and I saw genuine happiness, but that happiness had nothing to do with me. I was the one who was showing her something new. I'm the one who made her cum, without even touching her. That was all me. Does that count for anything? Do I get a smile and a glow, nope!

"I like him," she beamed.

"Don't get caught up on the first dick you slide down on."

"Damn, do you have to say it like that?"

"I am just speaking the truth. You're newly single and your ex, who isn't actually an ex-husband yet, just returned."

"That's right; I still hold that Negro's last name. Why can't a divorce just magically happen once one or both of the asses in the marriage decide to walk away? Why the entire preliminary shit? It's so that the courts and lawyers can earn money."

"Hey, I like how you said that," I laughed, trying to lighten the mood.

"He's cute." Natalie's eyes traveled past me as I looked over to see whom she was talking about.

I slid my tongue over the front of my teeth and hummed. He was a cutie all right; average height, caramel brown, pearly whites, curly hair, and some beautiful dark eyes. almost hypnotic. "He is yummy."

"Yummy isn't enough to describe that man."

I laughed as I finally downed my very own shot and then quizzed her, "Weren't you just goo-goo eyed over Silk?"

"But didn't you just tell me not to fall for the first dick that I slipped on madam?" She eyed me with her sarcastic grin.

I gently pushed her on her shoulder, brought my hand up to the back of her head, and rubbed it gently as I cradled it. "You want him?" I challenged.

She leans in closer to me. If you were looking at us from a distance, you would think that she was leaning in to kiss me as I held her head. "I want him," she whispered. The strong vapors of her alcohol were attacking my nostrils as I flinched to take the sting.

"You want him; then go get him."

She eyed me and laughed, "What do you mean, 'go get him'?"

"Don't get scared now, Ms. Plain Jane. Go after what you want," I teased.

"A man though?"

"He's just another guy. They are all the same and no different. Forget that myth that men have control over the pussy. We do. Women control if they will fuck us or not. Men are easy, not us."

"Men are easy?"

"Girl, let me put you on to some game. Society has this perception that women can't have random sex, because we are some emotional creatures who get unstable after we have let a man inside of us. And the kicker to me is that they want to put out into the atmosphere that we are the easy lays, when naturally, men are the hoes."

"I agree with the hoe part."

I continued, "Men cannot do what we don't want them to. And I promise you that if you don't want to fuck Mr. Sexy over there, then it won't happen. But if you do, then baby girl, you hold the power."

"Power?"

"The power of the punanny."

She raised her left eyebrow curiously as she leaned back into her seat and asked the bartender for another shot. "This could get interesting," she said just above a whisper.

I slyly watched her every move, not speaking, because it was clear that she was deep in thought. As she took the shot, she sat the glass back down and scooted towards the edge of her seat.

She grabbed my hand and said, "I have an idea. Dance with me on the dance floor."

"Oh, you're leading me," I joked, hopping out of my seat to follow behind her.

"For now I am. I want you to dance with me as I get Mr. Sexy's attention and once I do, I will switch up."

"You are sounding like a pro, Ms. Natalie."

She laughed, throwing her head back as we made our way onto the dance floor. "That I am, huh?"

She took my right hand and spun me in a full circle and we went into our groove, dancing to the latest hit. Our legs bent at the knees, our backs arched to create a round silhouette of our asses, and our arms were swinging in every direction.

I was really starting to like this chick. But unfortunately, she didn't understand just how much I liked her.

Chapter 19

Natalie

"Just give me all the loving. I'll do all the loving. I want to kiss you right there. That's all I ask of you." – Tony Toni Tone

"Tell me something," I whispered in his ear. "What is a man like you doing here...alone."

My hips were grinding in a slow seductive rhythm and I was certain that he was taking interest in what I was attempting to do. And that was to gain all of his attention. With his hands planted on my hips, he welcomed the motions my body created.

I turned my back to him and allowed myself to feel free. I pretended that this man was mine and that he was everything that I had ever wanted. I pretended that he was...Silk.

I was speechless.

Silk was on my mind in a moment when I wanted to be someone else; again. However, in this moment, I only wanted to be desired by a man who knew nothing of me, but the mere curves of my face as he first noticed them at hello. And Silk saw me and deep down that's one thing that scared me at this point in my life. I sought randomness from a guy in this moment and Silk was everything but random.

I shook the thoughts out of my head as I felt this mystery man's body near mine. He pressed himself up against me and a signal to wake up was sent to my clit to get my kitty's attention; I shivered.

You got my attention!

"I was waiting on a woman like you. A woman who seemed to know what she wanted," he replied.

"Oh yeah? And what do you think it is that I want from you?" I asked, allowing my head to fall back onto his shoulders as I turned my mouth towards his face for him to hear me. I bit my bottom lip at the end of my question to add a little more lust to it.

I could hear him moan and slightly grunt as he said, "Baby, you are sexy."

I smiled. "And you are sexy too, babe," I replied.

He began to hug me, wrapping his arms around my waist as he pulled me in closer to him. "You smell good."

We were still on the dance floor. Joyclyn had long gone to dance with someone new. Our seemingly routine dance earlier with one another caught us two fish. One for her and one for me. The game was on. I wanted him I thought, as I remembered the curve in his pink plump lips. I thought about his lips wrapped around my clit and shivered so hard you would have thought that I was cold.

"Take my hand; show me what it is you think that I want," I whispered in his ear.

He twirled me around in one big spin, and grabbed my hand as we proceeded to exit the dance floor. I looked around, finding Joyclyn off in the distance and waved goodbye. Sort of like a school-age girl who was asked out by the popular guy in   school, I was all giddy and whatnot.

***

We rushed into his condo after merely thirty minutes of kissing, sucking, and allowing him to finger my kitty as I rode in the passenger seat of his car. We were finally free of his vehicle and now had room to maneuver and tear clothing away from our bodies.

"I want to fuck you!" he growled in between our rough kisses.

No shit! I wanna fuck you too. Duh!

I ripped open his shirt as he pulled up my skirt, exposing my bare cheeks. He grabbed my ass with both hands and threw me in the air, wrapping my body around his. "Ahhh yes!" I cried.

"Fuck me babe. Fuck me!" I cried out again.

"Sexy...mother...fucker...you,"   he replied with so much passion as my hands madly ran over his bare back. My eyes were barely open as I halfway knew where we going. Up the stairs we went as he climbed them two at a time, with me wrapped around his body.

Oh shit, he is fit!

Witnessing him walk with me in his arms so freely up the stairs forced my kitty to gush. I was beyond ready to see what this man was going to do to me.

In his room on the eighth floor of this condominium; he had the large windows curtains pulled back and the nights skyline added to the way I was feeling right now. I just hoped that he wouldn't be a repeat of baby dick Dillan.

He threw me onto the bed as I allowed my body to fall limp onto his bedding. "Baby, you are beautiful," he said.

I smiled brightly as I bite my bottom lip. That bottom lip thing was becoming my signature calling. He takes a few steps back away from me and begins to unbuckle his pants. I became excited at his attempt of a strip tease. Yes! Let me see him, baby, I chanted in my head as I eyed his pants and watched the motions of his hands.

"You ready for me, baby?"

I nodded my head and then quietly replied, "Yes babe. I am so ready for you."

He slid his pants down and as he went to stand upright, I saw the bouncing of his black tool. Thick, dark, purple head and it was long; I just did a praise dance in my head.

My mouth hung open as this man confidently walked across his room, and opened his drawer to get that gold package. Unlike Dillan, this man should be honored with the gold package. I wanted to salute the brother for the great work he was about to do.

I watched closely as he ripped open the package and applied our protection. He looks back over to me and says in a demanding tone, "Why are you still dressed?"

I hopped up quickly like an anxious girl who'd just gotten reprimanded for not following directions and stripped my clothes away from my body in record time.

I stood before him naked as the day that I was born when he said, "Turn around. On your knees."

He was so stern and so demanding and I was nervous, but excited at the same time. I felt like a child being ordered around and that, for some reason had me all giddy. I obeyed his request, got on all fours, and tooted my ass in the air.

I could hear him walk up behind me as he slapped me hard on my ass. I could feel my ass jiggle as he moaned; a sound I was certain was approval as I winced at the discomfort, but welcomed gesture.

He took his hands, placing one on each cheek and parted them. He bends down, kissing my lower back, and then each cheek as I buried my face into his bedding. I felt him blow air on my asshole as I tighten up. He took his fingers and reached under, giving my clit a quick tug and then flicks it. I shivered.

"She ready for me?"

She? Ohh... my pussy! Yes! yes! "Yes, she's ready!"

I arched my back more as he tapped my inner thighs, signaling for me to open my legs wider. I obeyed. He took his hands to my ass cheeks again and as I felt the first initial touch of his dick on my pussy, I became weak with excitement. I was so excited that a new wave of juices formed around the walls of my pussy, and began to travel down the canal to greet his dick.

In one quick move, I took a deep breath as he entered me. I felt myself exhale as he began the initial stroking rhythms; I tightened my womb and took his size as if I was familiar with him.

"Ooo baby!" he moaned. I motioned with my hips, moving back and forth to match his rhythm. "That pussy is tight," He moaned, almost in a pleading and weak voice.

I threw myself into his body mass as we went at it, pacing that rhythm for the next twenty minutes. He was holding onto my waist as leverage, and I held onto his bed for balance.

And as if our bodies were used to one another, I felt our bodies tense up in an effort to mask the orgasmic rhythms that were quickly approaching. I screamed out as the pressure of my orgasm was difficult to mask quietly.

He collapsed on top of me as I fell onto his bed. There we lay, I being his cushion, his bed being mine, as our breathing was hot and heavy. "You are one amazing woman," he said, in between pants.

"You are amazing too..." I paused as I went to say his name, but realized I didn't know it. He picked up on my confusion and said, "Jason!"

"Jason!" I laughed, burying my face into his sheets. "Nice to meet you. I'm Jane."

He laughed and gave my ass three smacks. "Jane. Hmmmm, my Jane. Nice to have met you too, baby."

Chapter 20
Joyclyn

I lay on my back on my bed, opening the next bill for Joyclyn Jones and rolled my eyes. I hated this time of the month when bills were due and my bank account wasn't in agreement with me, or the fact that I needed money to pay them. I was broke, once more. Not because I was negligent; okay, whom am I kidding? I bought that Michael Kors bag for $800 to impress Shawn, my latest lay, but that Negro couldn't care less.

I thought about returning it, but shrugged that thought out of my head as I heard footsteps nearing my door. "Yeah!" I called out.

"Yo ma, are you up?"

I rolled my eyes, turning on my left side and blew out hot air. "Yep, that would be how I just spoke. What's up?"

My son Darius stood in my doorway. He was already two inches taller than I was, and at only twelve, I knew he would tower over six feet easily. I didn't hate my son, but I wouldn't be fooling anyone if I didn't admit that mother hood was a mistake for a woman like me.

"It's Saturday, are you going to take me to my friend's like you promised?" His voice was forever changing. I had to raise my head up from where it laid to ensure that it was actually him talking. Each day, it got deeper and deeper. He was becoming something I hated; a man.

"I forgot I said that. When are you trying to go?"

"Well, his pool party starts in an hour, please Ma I don't want to be the last one to show up."

I rolled my eyes. "And says the lame who wants to be the first to show up to a party," I laughed a little, tickled at the innocence he still possessed.

"Ma, it's just I want to be there for the whole thing," he argued.

I rose up again to look at him to see if he was pouting, because I could use a good laugh. But he wasn't. The only thing that I saw was the resemblance of his no-good daddy. I rolled my eyes and turned back over. "Go on and get dressed. I will get up in ten minutes."

I listened to him run off to his room, obviously to finish getting dressed as I rolled over onto the side of the bed and sat upright. I had a slight hangover from last night, when Natalie and I had gone out dancing and drinking. Although I hadn't heard from her since witnessing her leave the club with the cutie, I didn't worry about her. She seemed to be gaining her confidence in lighting speed.

I slipped on a sundress and wobbled out of my room, possessing the walk of a fat person; I was just naturally tired from last night. "Do you have the address?" I called out.

"Yes ma'am, here I come." I heard Darius call out from his room. I grabbed my car keys, phone, a quick yogurt out of the refrigerator and made my way out of our complex.

"Come on!" I called out just before the door closed behind me.

Half an hour later, Darius was out of sight and I was pulling up in the parking lot of the nearest McDonald's.

Hopping out to go inside to order, I hear someone call out to me, "Where are you headed to Ms. Lady?"

I turned around and recognized his voice on queue. "To pig out. The yogurt I just had isn't handling my hunger issues. What's up with you?"

I gave him a quick hug as we walked through the front doors together. "Nothing's up; worked up quite the appetite last night, so I am definitely cheating with a Big Mac."

"Hardy, har, har. So umm yeah; about last night, though. What's the scoop big daddy?" I asked laughingly as we both walked up to the counter and ordered our food.

"A chick that was down forever. I promise you; it's something about those chicks that have no bounds that is always bad news for my d..." His voice trailed off as he remembered that he was in public. "I mean, I am just weak for them, you know."

I laughed, understanding exactly what he meant. "And how was she? You know I am very aware of your skills, mister. You sir, have a very addictive, umm, member," I laughed, grabbing my cup from the cashier to go get my drink.

I walked over to the fountain and waited for him to join me. "So your plans to hit it panned out."

He gave me the blank stare as he playfully and seductively stood behind me, and wrapped his left arm around my waist as he got his drink with his right.

I purposely pushed my ass into his groin, feeling the slight hardness of his dick and giggled. "Oh yeah. You got what you wanted, I am certain of that."

I followed him over to a couple of chairs and took a seat. "This must be good. I had no intentions on sitting inside of a McDonald's to eat, but one must hear about last night though."

He scurried off to grab our food after hearing our numbers called and as he went to the condiments counter, I called out, " Jason, you better give me a handful of ketchup. And hurry up. I am dying to hear about Ms. Natalie."

Chapter 21
Silk

"It's about finding a new experience with someone you never thought you meet, who totally turns your life around completely, helping you get a job and keeping you off the streets, church on Sunday morning, eventually I'm saving money, sending my life in a new direction, now I'm friends with my old man again, standing here wearing this wedding band I can say I knew love because of you."-Anthony Hamilton

Centennial Park was my current location. I had set up a pallet with two blank canvases, some sandwiches, fruits, and some wine hidden in a tote bag; I had created a nice environment for Natalie today. It wasn't a special occasion or anything; I just wanted to see her smile.

"Very nice. Very, very nice, Silk," Natalie complimented me as she took a space on the blanket and took a look around at my set up. It was Wednesday; those who loved the arts, music, and a good time would always be in the park for the free Wednesday WindDown that Atlanta put on every Wednesday.

"A beautiful set up for a beautiful woman." I sat down next to her and leaned in as she accepted my kiss to her lips.

"You're a sweetie. I could get used to this," she said, eyeing the cut apples and then reaching for them.

"I have some sweet cream you can dip your fruit in as well," I handed her the white whipped cream as she tasted it and hummed.

"Good. Very good. So I see you have these canvases here. What are you painting today?"

I replied with, "We are going to create something together."

"Something like what?"

"I don't know. That's the thing; you can create whatever it is that you want.

The freedom of art baby!" I leaned in, kissing her lips again.

"I see!" She eyed the paint colors and then the brushes. "Can I create you?" she asked, looking directly at me. "I want to see what my hands will create in an effort to portray you."

I stared at her; in a way, she looked angelic to me. Angels were sometimes of the imagination and often in just a dream, but I felt that Natalie was just that; an angel. She was rare, beautiful, and a heavenly dream. She bit her bottom lip and smiled at me. Her rich brown eyes had a golden glow today. Maybe it was from the sun's reflection, but whatever it was, it seemed to enhance her beauty.

"That sounds like something worth painting." I managed to ignore my thoughts in a moment to reply to her. "Can I paint you?"

"I don't know you may make my nose too big." She laughed.

I laughed out, "Nah; I mean I may have to use some extra paint to get your forehead accurate, but I think we have enough here to cover that," I shot back as she threw an apple slice at me.

"Hey now, you have to give me a heads up if you're going to try and feed me food," I laughed out.

" Ha, ha, ha; very funny. It's on!"

"What's on?" I pretended to act clueless.

"The one who paints the other the best gets a full body massage. And FYI; I like oil, not lotion," she teased.

"Yeah, oil may work better on them ankles," I laughed out again.

"What!" Natalie laughed out, leaning in as she playfully punches my arm.

I pretend that I am in pain and cry out for her to stop. "Oh, you big baby!" She sucked her teeth and went to retrieve a paint brush.

"You're going to lose baby," I assured her.

She winked at me and said, "Either way, it's going to be an interesting night."

I nodded my head in agreement as the first drum sounds alerted us that the free concert was about to start. I grabbed a brush and my canvas and started the beginning touches of my Natalie portrait.

***

Hours had passed and we were laid across my couch. The sounds of the movie, Juice, played in the background as I looked down and noticed Natalie in a deep sleep. I managed to maneuver her from lying on top of me, so that I could move around a little.

Scooting to the edge of the couch, I leaned forward, placing my forearms on my knees and just sat there and stared. I couldn't explain this moment and why I felt weird. I wasn't upset or sad; I was just confused at how everything just seemed to be so good.

That sounds stupid, but it's true. Nothing was wrong in this moment. I was happy with where I was and it seemed that Natalie had come out of nowhere, but I knew that was a lie.

Maybe that's why I felt like this at this very moment. I knew that if the truth were to come out, then this happy feeling, this moment where it seemed like everything was perfect, would be non-existent.

I slowly rose up from the couch and found a nearby blanket to cover Natalie with, finally making my way into the kitchen to get a bottle of water. I downed half of its contents before taking a deep breath and leaning up against the counter.

Today was perfect. We listened to live music, drunk the wine, ate the food that I had packed, and Natalie managed to paint me into a stick figure. It was horrible, but how she made it seem like it was the best artwork ever created was hilarious. She was a cool woman to be around and cute at the same time. And then to top all of that, we had this sexual chemistry that was off the charts.

Why didn't I find this with her organically?

The buzzing of my phone on the kitchen table shook me out of my thoughts as I rushed over to it to quiet its sound before it woke Natalie.

I whispered into the device, "Hello!"

"Hey, Silky baby. What's up?"

I placed my hand over the phone as if Natalie could hear her voice through the receiver, while I snuck into the bathroom on my tiptoes. "Joyclyn, what are you doing calling me. You know I'm with Natalie."

"I know this, baby boy. Just seeing how everything is going on with you on your end. How's my plain Jane doing?"

"She's fine, Joy. What do I owe this phone call to?"

"I just wanted you to know our girl is getting a little reckless, just like I had planned."

I grew annoyed, but curious to know what she meant at the same time. "Reckless? In what way?"

"My boy Jason was deep in that, booboo. She's getting a little loose."

"Jason?" I cringed at the thought of someone else inside of her. How do you know?"

"I set it up, duh. Just as I did with you. She's making this easy." Joyclyn's laugh was evil and eerie. This chick is really crazy.

"Why throw him in the mix?"

"Do I sense a little jealousy over there? Have you gotten caught up, Silk baby?"

I ignored her question and asked, "Why are you calling me Joyclyn?"

"Just to say hello. Nothing major, boo."

"Okay cool then, because I have to go. No more men, Joy," I demanded.

"And why is that? Your girl is just now getting started. I think she wouldn't appreciate that request from you."

"You are something else." My voice was full of the sound of disgust. "Just calm it down on your end.

"Look, I have plans here; don't mess things up because you have caught feelings."

"Don't worry about me, I'm good," I shot back.

"Yeah, I can hear. You know you don't want to mess up our plans. Now do you?" I grew quiet. "I didn't think so. Well, off I go then. I'll chat with you later on, Silk." She hung up without my having to reply.

As I stood in the dark, empty, bathroom with only the moonlight, making its way through the blinds; I felt stuck. It wasn't a secret between Joyclyn and I that I was caught up and the fact that Natalie was just with another man ate at me.

Today, she'd acted as if I was her only one. Or maybe that's just what I wanted to think. Why do I care that I am not her only one? I shook my head and swung at the air. I was pissed. I felt stuck, lost, and then angry with myself for even getting caught up with Joyclyn, because now I knew that I would have to make a decision.

I knew that I was damn near loving Natalie. I wanted her. I loved everything about her. But she wasn't mine. She was a task that I had signed on to conquer, but ultimately she conquered me at first sight.

I turned on my heels to walk back into the living room to find Natalie still lying on the couch. I stared at her, watching the rise and fall of her chest and I felt myself sinking on the inside.

"I love you," I said, just above a whisper to a sleeping Natalie. She couldn't hear me, she didn't reply, but somewhere deep down inside of me, I wish she had heard me. I wish she knew the depths of my heart.

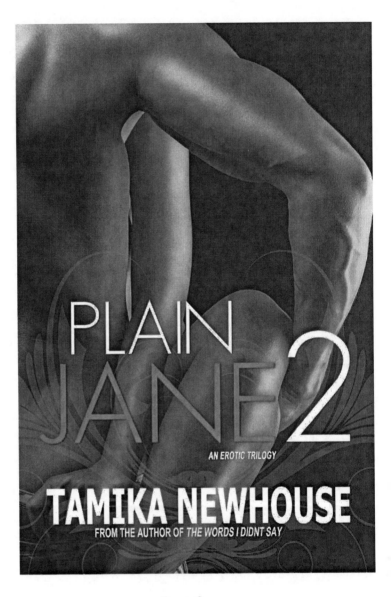

Part 2
Coming Fall 2015

CPSIA information can be obtained
at www.ICGtesting.com
Printed in the USA
LVOW10s1855020317
525948LV00011B/774/P